HOBBIES AND HOMICIDE
A DUNE HOUSE COZY MYSTERY
BOOK TWENTY-FIVE

CINDY BELL

**Copyright © 2023 Cindy Bell
All rights reserved.**

All rights reserved. No part of this publication may be reproduced or transmitted in any form or by any means, electronic or mechanical, including photocopy, recording, or any information storage or retrieval system, without permission in writing from the publisher.

This is a work of fiction. The characters, incidents and locations portrayed in this book and the names herein are fictitious. Any similarity to or identification with the locations, names, characters or history of any person, product or entity is entirely coincidental and unintentional.

All trademarks and brands referred to in this book are for illustrative purposes only, are the property of their respective owners and not affiliated with this publication in any way. Any trademarks are being used without permission, and the publication of the trademark is not authorized by, associated with or sponsored by the trademark owner.

ISBN: 9798391915829

CHAPTER 1

Mary Brent scooped up the orange peels from the counter and dropped them into a compost container. Tension built up in her muscles at the thought of what the next hour might bring. She'd let Suzie Allen talk her into something that she didn't think would end well.

"I'm just not sure that I'll be able to handle it, Suzie." Mary glanced down at her knees, currently covered by thin, blue jeans.

"I promise, she'll be able to help you modify the exercises to make it more comfortable. I really think that it might actually help you to get a little more flexibility and maybe relieve some of your discomfort." Suzie poured fresh orange juice into a glass. "I can't believe you made this yourself."

"Well, Michael and Molly mentioned that they really enjoyed orange juice for breakfast, so I thought it would be a nice touch." Mary smiled as she placed toasted bagels onto plates. "I just want everyone to feel comfortable here, and since we only have a few guests this weekend, it's easy to give a little extra. I'm sure the other guests will enjoy some as well."

"You're so great at all of this." Suzie poured herself a cup of coffee. "You never miss a single detail."

"Neither do you." Mary gestured to the kitchen décor that surrounded them. "Your interior design skills make this place come alive with warmth. I never would have thought to add a slightly brighter color above the cabinets to give the whole place a glow."

"I do like it." Suzie glanced along the top of the cabinets as she smiled. "I guess we both have our own strengths when it comes to running this B&B. That's why we make the perfect team."

"That, and a lifetime of friendship." Mary picked up her own cup of coffee and held it out toward Suzie's.

"Yes, I'll always toast to that." Suzie touched her

mug against Mary's as she grinned. "I just hope our friendship survives yoga."

At the sound of the front door opening, they turned toward it.

"Morning," Michael called out as he walked into the kitchen with his wife, Molly. The couple, who were in their fifties, were staying at Dune House for the weekend to celebrate their wedding anniversary.

"Oh, this looks amazing." Molly smiled.

"It does." Michael looked over at the food spread out on the table.

"Have you already been out this morning?" Mary asked.

"Yes, we couldn't sleep and wanted an early start." Molly wrung her hands. "It was so beautiful on the beach. It's such an amazing setting."

"We love it here." Mary poured some orange juice into glasses.

"Once you've finished your breakfast, we can head down to yoga." Suzie looked between them.

"Oh." Molly glanced at her husband.

"Thank you, but we've changed our minds." Michael cleared his throat. "We're going to skip it. We might have a rest after breakfast."

"Okay." Suzie was surprised. They seemed eager

to join them when she had told them about the yoga classes the previous evening.

"My back is playing up, so we thought we would give it a miss." Molly held her hands above her head and arched her back to stretch it. "It often gives me trouble."

"That's no good." Suzie frowned.

"Why don't you relax on the porch, and I'll bring this all out to you?" Mary waved her hand over the orange juice and bagels. "The chairs are very comfortable."

"Thank you." Michael started toward the door.

After Suzie and Mary set up everything on the table outside, they walked back into the kitchen.

"Well, they seem happy with breakfast." Mary smiled.

"They do. Come on, we need to get ready for yoga on the beach."

"What's this I hear about yoga on the beach?" Jeanette grinned as she walked into the kitchen. Wavy black hair, held back by a hair tie, cascaded down her back to reach her waistline. Her running clothes accentuated her slender but muscular figure.

"You're invited. It's just a little farther along the beach." Suzie pointed in the direction. "I only found out about it after you went to your room last night, and I didn't want to interrupt you." She handed her a plate with the bagel on it, while Mary offered her the glass of orange juice. "It starts in about thirty minutes, plenty of time to eat breakfast before we head out."

"Oh, this is so sweet of you." Jeanette took a sip of the orange juice, then set the glass down. "But I can't eat or drink anything but water before my run. I need to run on an empty stomach. I'm sorry, I should have mentioned that. I will definitely enjoy this later, though."

"I didn't know you were a runner." Suzie smiled. "It's a beautiful morning for it."

"Great, I can't wait to get out there. If I get back in time, I'll definitely join you for the yoga class." Jeanette tucked earbuds into her ears as she walked out of the kitchen and into the dining room. Sliding glass doors led out to a wraparound porch. The porch led straight out onto the beach.

"Wow, I wish I had that much enthusiasm in these old bones." Mary gave a short laugh.

"Mary, you're not old. Yoga is great at any age, you're going to feel so good after."

"I never knew you were such a proponent of it. How did I miss that?"

"You didn't. I did it for a little while during my

travels to help me wake up in the morning. But I fell out of the habit pretty quickly. I do recall it being very good for me, though, and I'm eager to get back into it." Suzie settled her hands on Mary's shoulders and looked into her eyes. "Trust me. Just go get changed, and we can head down early to do some stretching. I'm sure Lizzy will help you through it every step of the way."

"Lizzy, the twenty-two-year-old yoga instructor, is going to help me with these worn-out knees?" Mary smacked one of her knees as she smiled. "I think she might be getting more than she bargained for."

"Oh, Mary." Suzie placed her hands on her hips as she studied her. "One of these days you're going to know just how amazing you are."

"I doubt it's going to be during yoga." Mary waved over her shoulder as she walked toward the stairs that led to her room. Dune House had three floors. Most of the rooms offered stunning views of the beach.

When Mary and Suzie first teamed up to turn the home Suzie had inherited from her uncle back into a bed and breakfast, Suzie had decorated each room with a different theme and changed them regularly.

Suzie took care of the decorating and most of the admin, while Mary manned the kitchen, and they shared the housework. Working with her best friend felt like a dream. They had their conflicts now and then, but they always resolved them.

Mary looked at her reflection in the mirror that hung on the back of her door. She'd spent a lifetime with doubts about her figure, especially after having two children. She'd always had some extra pounds and considered her features to be plain. When she turned forty, a few gray strands showed up in her auburn hair. Now, in her fifties, they were scattered throughout. She didn't mind it. But after putting on the clothes that Suzie picked out for her yoga experience, the old habit of criticizing what she saw surfaced.

"Ugh, enough of this!" She stepped away from the mirror and grabbed a hair tie to pull her hair back with. Once she had it in a tight ponytail, she stepped out of her room.

Suzie flounced past her in bright pink leggings paired with a fluorescent-orange, off-the-shoulder workout top. Her brassy-blonde hair bounced around her cheeks as she spun around toward Mary.

"What do you think?" She grinned. "I dug it out of the back of my closet."

"I think you look amazing." Mary laughed. "And you'll be very easy to spot."

"A bit much, right?" Suzie laughed. "But I thought it would be fun. You look fantastic."

"Should we bring Pilot down with us? I think he'd be well-behaved."

The yellow Lab, who was curled up on his bed in the foyer near the front door, jumped up and ran toward them at the sound of his name.

"Hmm, maybe instead of goat yoga, he could do dog yoga?" Suzie grinned as she pet the top of Pilot's head. "But he might be a bit big for that."

"You're right. He might be well-behaved, but it could be distracting if he tries to join in." Mary laughed as she imagined it.

"Are you ready?"

"As I'll ever be." Mary groaned.

"Where's that sunny disposition that always gets me going in the morning?" Suzie winked at her. "You're usually the one telling me to think positive."

"I'm positive. I'm just positive that this is going to hurt." Mary followed Suzie out through the sliding glass doors. They led Pilot to the fenced yard and threw the ball to him, which he eagerly retrieved and dropped at their feet. "We won't be long." Mary patted Pilot's head, then closed the gate.

"Seriously, though, Mary, if you do feel it's too much, just let me know and we can both just go for a walk on the beach." Suzie looped her arm through Mary's.

Suzie felt a cool breeze blow off the surface of the water as they walked farther down the beach.

"Actually, maybe a walk is the way to go. It's such a gorgeous morning. Not too hot, not too cool, it's perfect."

"No, Suzie, I don't want you to miss out because of me."

"I won't be missing out. I'll be getting to spend some time with you." Suzie nudged her shoulder. "Relax, we're going to have a good morning, no matter what. I can feel it." She took a deep breath of the morning air, laced with just a touch of salt, and listened to the crashing waves in the distance.

As they walked down the beach, Suzie scanned the expanse farther ahead of her and discovered brightly colored yoga mats set up on the sand not far from the edge of the ocean. Beyond them, a woman in workout gear knelt down in the sand near the water.

"Oh, Lizzy's already set up." Suzie smiled as she approached the yoga teacher who had invited them to the class. "Are you ready?"

"As ready as I'll ever be."

"Lizzy!" Suzie called out as she approached her, but she didn't respond.

The water that lapped around the woman's bare feet had an unusual tint. The sight of it took Suzie's breath away.

"Is that blood?" Mary stared at the water.

"Are you okay, Lizzy?" Suzie gasped.

"She's dead." Lizzy turned to look at them with wide eyes and a cold voice. "I thought I could help, but she's dead."

Suzie looked beyond Lizzy and saw a body half-in and half-out of the water. A woman in a T-shirt and shorts. Beside her, mostly in the water, was a metal detector. Suzie's gaze shifted back to the woman in the water. Clearly, she was dead. The wound on her head left no question about that. It looked like she had been hit with the metal detector. She had been murdered!

CHAPTER 2

"Lizzy, come away from there." Mary gestured for Lizzy to join her. "Come here, come away from there. Did you call the police?"

Suzie knew the woman in the water was dead, but she needed to make sure. She crouched down and carefully leaned forward so she didn't fall in the water. She felt for a pulse on the woman's neck. As she suspected, there wasn't one.

"No, I had just found her when you came here." Lizzy's voice wavered, and she started sobbing, as if the reality of the situation suddenly dawned on her. "I was so shocked, I didn't know what was going on." She turned into Mary's arms and rested her head against her shoulder.

"I'll call Jason." Suzie's voice barely raised above the sound of the crashing waves.

Concern washed over Suzie as she looked over at her friend. Mary patted Lizzy's back while Suzie summoned Detective Jason Allen. As much as Suzie didn't want to look, she felt her gaze being pulled back to the person in the water. Something about her looked familiar. All at once, she recognized her as one of the women she often saw on the beach with a group of three other people.

"She's new to the area, but she's a local." Suzie drew a breath to calm her rattled nerves. "Her name is Kendra."

"I can hear the sirens." Lizzy pulled away from Mary and looked toward the parking lot. "But it's too late. It's not like they can help her." Tears began to slide down her cheeks again. "It's too late."

"They might not be able to save her, but they can catch whoever did this to her." Mary's voice grew determined. "It's important to find out what happened."

"Yes, I suppose it is." Lizzy took a step away from Suzie and Mary. "I shouldn't be here. I should go."

"Go?" Suzie looked at Lizzy. "What do you mean?"

"I'm sorry, I'm just really upset, and I need to get out of here." Lizzy started to gather her belongings.

"You can't go." Suzie stepped in front of her, her tone stern. "You're the only witness. You have to stay and talk with the police."

"I'm not a witness." Lizzy reeled back and dropped her purse in the process. "I told you, I didn't see anything. I only saw her after I finished setting everything up."

"Lizzy." Mary spoke in a soothing tone. "It's okay, we know that you had nothing to do with this. But you may know more than you think. You might have heard or seen something that will help the investigation, and they know the right questions to ask you to find out. It's really important that you tell them everything you know."

"I don't want to." Lizzy's voice took on a petulant tone as she backed away.

"Lizzy." Suzie stepped toward her. "This isn't the time to panic. We need to help make sure her murderer is caught."

"Murderer," Lizzy repeated the word as she shivered. She squeezed her eyes shut, then slowly nodded. "Yes. You're right. Of course, I'll stay. I'm sorry." She opened her eyes again and sighed. "I'm just so shocked. I've never seen anything like this in my life. I can't stop shaking."

Mary wrapped her arm around her.

"It's okay. We're here with you."

Suzie stepped up on the other side of her and took her hand.

"You're not alone, Lizzy. We'll help you through speaking with the police and make sure that you have everything that you need."

"It was supposed to be my first class." Lizzy sniffled as she stared down at a yoga mat unfurled on the sand. "It was supposed to be a new start."

"You'll still get to have that first class." Mary rubbed the back of her hand. "It's just not going to be today."

Sirens blared as police cars pulled into the parking lot of the beach. Seconds later, Jason came into view.

"Suzie, Mary, are you okay?" He jogged toward them with a couple of police officers following him.

Suzie met her cousin's eyes.

"We're okay. Just in shock." She glanced over her shoulder at the body. "I just checked for a pulse. But aside from that, we haven't touched her."

"Good." Jason surveyed the scene and checked

the body, then he gestured to a young officer who stepped up behind him. Officer Beth Chambers. "Beth, get some cones, and make sure no one comes down this way." He turned toward Detective Kirk Rondella who stood beside him. "Kirk, I need you to contact Summer and get her out here as soon as possible."

Dr. Summer Rose was the local medical examiner and Jason's wife.

"Yes, sir." Kirk's gaze settled on the body. "Should we pull her out of there? The water is going to destroy the evidence."

"Not yet. I need to get some pictures of her positioning and make sure we're not going to disturb any evidence." Jason pulled his phone out of his pocket. He looked over at the group still huddled together. "Who found her?"

Lizzy squeaked. She squeezed her eyes shut again.

"Lizzy found her." Mary rubbed her arm. "She's pretty overwhelmed right now. Suzie and I came down here shortly after Lizzy found her."

"Lizzy. I'm Detective Jason Allen." Jason's tone softened as he studied the woman. "Anything you can tell me might be helpful."

"How?" Lizzy stared over at the body. "She's dead. Nothing can help that!"

"That may be true, but we need to find out who did this to her." Jason met her eyes. "Can I get your full name?"

"Elizabeth Kale," Lizzy stumbled over her words. "I can't do this. How can she be dead?"

"Just try to take a few slow breaths. Very gentle, in and out." Mary modeled the slow breathing.

"How can I?" Lizzy's breathing quickened. She pressed her hand against her chest. "I think I'm having a heart attack!"

Suzie's chest tightened as she watched Lizzy gasp for breath.

"Lizzy, it's probably a panic attack." Suzie rubbed her hand along her back. "Close your eyes, and just focus on breathing."

Jason pulled his radio from its holster and called for paramedics.

"We have help on the way to check you out." Jason watched as Suzie continued to try to soothe Lizzy. "Are you feeling any better?"

"Yes, a little." Lizzy let out a deep breath. "I'm sorry, I was probably just panicking."

"It's to be expected in a situation like this." Mary

gestured to a dune closer to the house. "Why don't you come sit down? That might help."

"All right, yes, let's try that." Lizzy took a deep breath as she allowed Mary to guide her to the dune.

Suzie stepped in front of Lizzy to block her view of the body that Beth and Kirk had begun guarding.

CHAPTER 3

"Lizzy." Jason walked over to her. "I need you to answer a few questions for me. Do you think you can do that?"

"Please. Just tell me what happened." Lizzy looked up at Jason. "Who did this? Who would do this? I did an energetic cleansing before I came here. I tried to make sure the air would be clear and full of light and love. Why did this happen? Who would murder her?"

Jason glanced over at Suzie and Mary, then looked back at Lizzy.

"I don't know, but I intend to find out. I know this is quite a shock, but you were the first person on the scene. You might have noticed something that could help find the murderer. I need you to answer a few questions for me."

"Get it together." Beth stepped between Jason and Lizzy and clicked her fingers right in front of Lizzy's face. "You have a duty to this woman to answer our questions!"

"Beth!" Kirk snapped. "She's not in any state to answer questions right now. She needs to calm down first."

A few people began walking toward the beach from the parking lot.

"The other students are arriving for the class." Mary pointed toward them. "They shouldn't see this."

"I'll stay with Lizzy. You secure the beach." Jason looked at Beth and Kirk. "Not a word to anyone about what's happened. We need to get what details we can before the rumors start."

"Understood, sir." Kirk gave a short nod.

"Are you sure you don't want me to stay with Lizzy? I can probably get her talking." Beth looked at Jason.

"We're not interrogating her, Beth." Jason's patient tone took on a faint edge of annoyance.

"Why not? She's the one who was found with

the victim. She should be our top suspect." Beth glared at him.

"What?" Lizzy wailed. "You think I did this?" Fresh tears began flowing. "Are you going to arrest me?"

"Beth!" Jason's sharp tone cut through the chaos and commanded attention. "Go with Kirk."

Beth quickly followed after Kirk. The flush in her cheeks indicated she realized her mistake.

Jason shifted his gaze toward a woman jogging down the beach in their direction.

"Do you know this person?"

"It's Jeanette." Mary stepped forward and waved to Jeanette. "She's one of our guests for the weekend."

"Okay, I'd like to speak with her." Jason pulled his notepad out of his pocket.

"I'll stay with Lizzy." Suzie wrapped her arm around Lizzy's shoulders.

Jeanette slowed to a stop as Mary continued to wave to her.

"Did I make it in time for the class?" Jeanette smiled as she pulled her earbuds from her ears. They dangled down around the necklace that she wore. Her gaze scanned the area, then shifted to

Jason as he stepped up beside Mary. "Is something wrong? Why are the police here?"

"I'm sorry, Jeanette, but there has been a terrible tragedy," Mary said.

"I'm Detective Jason Allen. Can I get your full name?" Jason poised his pen above his notepad.

"Jeanette Winters. What's happened?" Jeanette took a step toward him.

"A body has been discovered. We need confirmation but we suspect she was murdered." Jason locked his eyes to hers. "Did you hear anything? A scream? A fight? Anything at all? No detail is too small."

"What?" Jeanette stammered as she glanced in the direction of the crime scene. "Someone is dead?"

"Yes." Jason tapped his pen against his notepad as he continued to study her. "We need to find out as much information as possible about what's happened, as soon as possible. If you were out jogging when this happened, you might know something relevant."

"I'm sorry, but I don't. I ran all the way to the woods." Jeanette gestured to her ear. "I had my earbuds in the whole time. I didn't hear anything."

"Did you see anyone on the beach maybe?" Jason made a note on his notepad.

"No, no one. But to be honest, I wasn't really paying attention. When I run, I get a little lost in my head. I'm so sorry, I wish I had more to tell you." Jeanette looked over at Suzie and Mary as she fiddled with her necklace. "Were you two here when it happened? Are you okay?"

"We're okay." Suzie smiled slightly. "We weren't here, yet. It looks like maybe no one was around at the time."

"We know that at least one person was." Mary looked around. "Whoever killed her."

"Yes." Lizzy suddenly spoke up. "Yes, you're right. And that person was probably here not too long before I walked down here. Right? She didn't look like she'd been there long. Did she?" She looked at Jason.

"No, not too long. Tests need to be done, but I would say she died within the last hour or so." Jason held her gaze. "So, please, try to think about what it was like when you walked down here. Did you notice anything? Hear anything?"

"No, nothing. It's my first class. I tried to calm my nerves before it, so I went for a walk along the beach when I first got here, in the other direction of the parking lot." Lizzy pointed in that direction. "I was focusing on the water, trying to relax. I didn't notice anything. Then, when I went back to get my stuff and walked here, I was so focused on what I was doing. I had so much to carry. I didn't notice anything else." She wiped tears from her cheeks. "I'm sorry."

"It's okay." Mary patted her shoulder. "That's a good start. You should both come back to Dune House and get some water, or some tea. Once you calm down, you may start to remember something else."

"Jason?" Suzie looked over at him. "Would that be okay with you? It might help to be in a different setting."

"All right, you four go ahead back, and I'll meet up with you there later. Summer should be here soon." Jason looked at Lizzy and Jeanette. "Thank you both for your help."

As Jason walked off toward the body, Mary thought about Lizzy's words. She had made a good point. The killer might have been on the beach just a few minutes before any of them had arrived. If things had been just a little different, any one of them could have encountered the murderer. Maybe, if she had been there sooner she could have done something to help, or maybe she would have been another victim. She watched as Jeanette and Lizzy began to walk ahead of her toward Dune House. They had both been alone on the beach, perfect victims. The quicker the murderer was found, the better.

CHAPTER 4

"Please! Just let us through!" A tall, slender woman tried to push past Kirk and Beth at the end of the beach. "Please! Is it true? Is it Kendra?"

Suzie looked toward the commotion and scanned the faces of the three people who demanded to get closer to the crime scene. She recognized them from their morning excursions on the beach.

Suzie had met Leanne, Larry, and Will, in passing while walking Pilot on occasion. They had never had a proper conversation but often exchanged small talk.

"Jason, those three people are also often out here with their metal detectors." Suzie glanced over at him. "It might be a good idea to talk with them."

"Oh, yes, of course. I know them." Jason waved to Kirk and Beth to allow the three through. He walked across the beach toward them.

"It's true, isn't it?" Larry, the taller of the two men, who looked to be in his forties, spoke in a deep, sorrow-filled voice. "She's gone?"

"A woman has died, but we haven't identified her, yet." Jason looked between the three of them. "You think it might be your friend Kendra?"

"It must be." Leanne stared at him. "She's not answering her phone."

"What is her full name?" Jason asked.

"Kendra Walkers," Leanne said.

"Did she tell you she would be out on the beach today?" Jason searched her eyes.

"This is her usual time." Will, who was at least twenty years older than the other two, shrugged. "I doubt it would be anyone else."

"But it could be, right?" Leanne's voice pitched higher with a mixture of hope and desperation.

"Did you know Kendra well?" Jason made a note on his notepad.

"Did we?" Leanne gasped as she tried to peer past Jason, toward the area of the beach that had been blocked off with a white tarp. "You said, 'did we' not 'do we.' Is it true, then? Is she really gone?"

"Tell us," Will demanded. "We have a right to know what happened to Kendra. She's our friend."

"I understand that." Jason looked at each of them in turn. "She didn't have any identification on her. But if any of you feels up to it, I can show you a picture to see if you can identify her. It won't be easy to look at."

"I'll do it." Leanne stepped forward. "Show me."

"Leanne, are you sure?" Larry touched her arm and met her eyes.

"Yes, I'm sure." Leanne leaned on his arm as Jason held up the phone. "Oh my, yes! That's Kendra!" She clapped her hand over her mouth as her eyes widened. "She didn't just die, did she?" She stared at Jason, her voice trembled as she spoke.

"I'm so sorry to tell all of you this, but from what we can tell so far, we believe Kendra was murdered. It didn't happen too long ago." Jason studied each of their faces in turn.

Suzie tightened her grasp on Mary's arm as she whispered to her, "You'd better take Lizzy and Jeanette up to the house. I'll stay here to see if Jason has any more questions for me."

"Okay, you're right." Mary guided Jeanette and Lizzy farther up the beach.

"No! She can't be dead!" Larry shouted and

started to push past Jason. "I don't believe it! Let me see her!"

"You can't." Jason easily held him back. "I'm sorry, but you can't. What you can do is help me to understand more about Kendra and who might have done this to her."

"Stop, Larry, just stop." Will put his hands on Larry's shoulders. "There's nothing you can do now. Seeing it won't make it any easier."

"I can't believe she's gone!" Leanne covered her mouth as a moan escaped it. "She was killed? By who?"

"That's what we're trying to find out now. You can help me with that, by telling me every detail you can about Kendra." Jason looked over at Leanne. "Can you tell me how you knew Kendra, Leanne?"

"We were friends. I haven't known her for too long, she moved here about a month ago. But she joined our metal-detecting club. It's just me and Larry and Will. We all became friends."

"She called me this morning," Larry whispered as he stared down at the sand. "She asked me to come out with her. But I couldn't. I had work to catch up on. Why didn't I just say yes? If I had said yes, she might still be alive."

"You can't blame yourself." Leanne looked over

at him. "None of us went with her this morning, Larry. She chose to go out on her own. She could have stayed home."

"Did she normally go out on her own? Was it unusual for her to be on the beach alone?" Jason looked up from his notepad.

"We have a policy that we should work in pairs whenever possible. It's just a safety rule. But Kendra always did exactly what she wanted. It's not the first time she's gone out on her own, and not the only rule she's broken," Will said.

"Hush, Will, now is not the time." Larry shot a sharp look in his direction. "Have some respect."

"As I said, every detail is important." Jason looked from Larry, back to Will. "What rules did she break?"

Will met Larry's eyes and shook his head.

"Nothing important." Will shrugged.

"Are you sure about that?" Jason narrowed his eyes.

"Yes." Will nodded.

"Do you know if Kendra had any issues with anyone recently? Was there anyone in her life that she was at odds with?" Jason looked back at Larry.

"Not that I know of. No. She didn't really seem

to know too many people. Certainly no one that wanted to hurt her," Larry said.

"She was a good person. She didn't have any enemies. She didn't do anything to deserve this." Leanne shivered.

"I'm sure she didn't." Jason's tone softened. "I'm sorry for your loss. If you think of anything that might be important to the investigation, please contact me right away." He handed them each one of his business cards. "If she had family issues, or a run-in with someone, anything like that might be helpful. Or even if she just seemed to be acting differently recently. Nothing is too small to mention."

"We'll take some time to think about it and let you know." Leanne stared at the crime scene once more, then signaled to Larry and Will. "There's nothing we can do here. Let's let the police do their work."

They turned and walked back toward the parking lot.

Suzie stared after them as Jason came to stand beside her.

"Are you really just going to let them leave?"

"Right now, I have no other option." Jason made another note on his notepad. "But I will definitely be looking into them and question them more. I think there is a lot they're not saying."

"Sometimes friends can turn out to be your greatest enemies." Suzie crossed her arms. "I think Leanne was hiding something. Something about her just seems a little off, and Larry tried to keep Will quiet."

"We'll find out soon enough. I've known Leanne and Larry for years. They've always been friendly. Of course, that doesn't mean they aren't hiding something. At least I have a full name now. That will get us started." Jason walked off to join Kirk and Beth.

Suzie spotted the medical examiner's van pull up in the parking lot. Summer stepped out, wearing her long, white lab coat. She clutched a black bag in one hand as she hurried down the beach, toward the crime scene.

"Summer!" Jason walked toward her and met her just as she reached the police tape.

"What a way to start the morning." Summer lifted the tape above her head.

Suzie lingered just outside the police tape and tried to hear what they were saying.

"What can you tell me?" Summer glanced at Jason.

"Deceased female. About thirty. It doesn't look like she's been here long." Jason walked beside her. "She was found floating in the water, but it looks like she was killed by the damage done from multiple blows to her head by a metal detector."

"Do you have a name, yet?" Summer looked at Jason.

"Kendra Walkers," Jason said.

"All right." Summer walked behind a screen that had been set up to protect Kendra from view.

For the moment, Kendra's death remained a mystery, and the fact that a murderer might still be roaming the beach, sent a shiver up Suzie's spine. She suddenly felt the urge to get back to Dune House.

CHAPTER 5

When Mary returned to Dune House, she let Pilot inside. As she walked past the reception desk, she found a note. It was from Molly and Michael saying that they had to leave urgently. They had a family emergency. They apologized and thanked Suzie and Mary for a wonderful time.

"Oh, I hope everyone's okay," Mary muttered to herself. After getting Lizzy and Jeanette settled in the living room, she went to check Michael and Molly's room. Everything seemed tidy, and their stuff was gone.

Mary didn't want to make a noise and wake their other guest, Josh, in case he was still sleeping.

Josh was moving to the neighboring town of Parish from the West Coast. He was in his early twenties and staying at Dune House while he was waiting to take over the lease of an apartment in a couple of weeks. He had gotten a job as a chef at a small Italian restaurant in Parish and often worked late and slept in.

Mary came downstairs and filled the teakettle with water. As she did, she heard someone descend the stairs behind her.

"Josh, I thought maybe you were still asleep?"

"No, I've been up for a while. I have to get to work. I'm covering lunch and dinner, today." Josh ran his hand through his blond curls. "I just got a text from Larry, my friend in town. Apparently someone was murdered on the beach? Kendra?"

"Yes. It's so terrible. We were down there shortly after she was found," Mary stumbled over her words. "Did you know Kendra?"

"No, not really. I just met her a couple of times in passing. I can't believe she was murdered."

"I know. It's shocking." Mary's first way to offer comfort was always through food. "Do you want some tea or crackers or anything? A bagel?"

"No, but thank you. I have to get to work." Josh started toward the back door.

Mary watched Josh leave, then her attention was drawn to the conversation in the dining room.

"I'm still having a hard time believing any of this is real," Jeanette said.

"It is. I know it's real. I saw her. I also can't believe it." Lizzy's voice trembled.

Mary listened to Lizzy's shock, and Jeanette's disbelief carry into the kitchen from the dining room.

Mary set the teakettle on the stove to heat and gathered some cookies, crackers, and cheese to fill a platter with. As she arranged the snacks, her heart pounded with a strange rhythm. Each beat felt out of place. Someone had been murdered just down the beach from Dune House. She hadn't heard anything unusual, and yet as she was getting ready to participate in a yoga class, Kendra had been murdered.

The whistle of the teakettle disrupted her thoughts. She poured the water into the three cups she had placed on a tray, along with cream, sugar, and an assortment of tea bags. As she carried the tray into the dining room, she heard Suzie's confident voice.

"I just wanted to let you both know the medical examiner has arrived on the scene, and soon they will have a lot more information about the murder. Jason and his officers will get to the bottom of this. That much I know for sure. It may not bring Kendra back, but knowing who committed the murder will at least give us all some peace of mind." Suzie met Mary in the doorway of the kitchen and the dining room and took the tray from her. "Thank you so much, Mary. This is perfect." She set the tray down on the dining room table.

Mary felt some relief, as her hands were still shaking a bit from the shock of the morning's events, and part of her had expected to spill the tea everywhere. Suzie was great at handling a crisis. Mary turned back to the kitchen to get another cup and the food and nearly tripped over Pilot, who had curled up between the kitchen and the dining room.

"Pilot, what are you doing, you silly dog?" Mary laughed. "You almost tripped me!"

The yellow Lab wagged his tail as he picked up his head to look up at her.

"Give me a second. I'll get you a treat." Mary edged around him and retrieved the cup and platter from the kitchen. When she returned, Pilot stood up and walked along beside her until she reached a chair to sit in. Mary gave him a couple of crackers.

When she sat down, he rested his head in her lap, and she stroked the top of his head as she tuned into the conversation happening around her.

"I'm sorry, I know I'm a mess. I just can't stop crying." Lizzy pressed a tissue against her nose as she sniffled. "Every time I think I can stop, I see her in that water again. I don't think I'll ever be able to forget."

"I just can't listen to this anymore." Jeanette bolted up out of her chair. "I know that's rude of me, but I'm not from here. I didn't know the woman who died, and as much as this is clearly a tragedy, I really don't want to have to listen to this."

"Of course." Mary looked up at her with an understanding nod. "Just let us know if you need anything."

"Thanks." Jeanette picked up her cup of tea. "And thanks for the tea." She crossed through the living room in the direction of the stairs that led up to the second floor.

"I'm sorry, I didn't mean to run her off." Lizzy sniffled. "I just can't calm down. I'm being selfish, I know. But I just started my business here. I'm afraid that after this, no one is going to want to come near my classes. I advertise it as a peaceful, inspirational experience. But now everyone is going to think of someone being murdered instead of the spiritual, refreshing experience it's supposed to be. It's going to ruin me! How am I going to pay my rent?"

"I know this feels very overwhelming right now." Suzie gently pushed her tea toward her. "Try to drink a little. It will help."

"How?" Lizzy stared down at the tea. "How can this help? How can anything help?"

"You would be surprised how much just some companionship after a shock like this can help." Mary reached across the table and took her hand. "You're part of our community now, Lizzy, and we're going to support you."

"Really?" Lizzy looked up from her tea with a faint smile. "Do you mean that?"

Mary gazed back at her with a slow nod.

"Yes, of course. It wasn't that long ago that Suzie and I were brand new to this community, too, but the people here welcomed us. I know it can seem intimidating at first, but trust me, it's a great place to live."

"Not for Kendra, though," Lizzy muttered as she looked back down at her tea.

Mary's lips tightened.

Suzie cleared her throat.

"Let's try not to focus on that right now. What happened to Kendra was unfortunate, but there's a good chance someone from out of town committed the crime. Kendra was new to town as well."

"She was?" Lizzy took a sip of her tea, then set it back down. "I wonder if she might have been planning to join my yoga class. I left the invitation open in my advertisements. I didn't require anyone to sign up. I just listed a time and a location and said that everyone would be welcome."

"How exactly did you advertise the class?" Mary leaned forward.

"Online, mostly. I don't have a big budget for even printing out flyers. But I made sure that I put it out there on every local social media page. Why?" Lizzy asked.

"Can you send me a link to what you posted?" Mary picked up her phone.

"Sure." Lizzy picked up her own phone. "It's just a picture of the beach and the details about the class."

Mary's phone buzzed with the text. She opened the photograph and noticed a few people in the background. She spread her fingertips across the picture causing it to enlarge. A moment later, her eyes widened and her mouth dropped open.

"Mary?" Suzie stood up from her chair and walked over to her. "What's wrong?"

"It's her." Mary pointed to the phone. "In the picture. It's Kendra."

"What?" Lizzy bolted out of her chair and rounded Mary's chair to peer at the picture. "No way. That's not possible."

"It does look like her. She even has the same top on." Suzie held up the phone in Lizzy's direction. "Did you know that you took her picture?"

"No, of course not! I mean, it was a beautiful morning, and there were a few people on the beach. I didn't really think about who was in the picture, I just snapped a shot to post." Lizzy squeezed her eyes shut. "This is crazy! But it's just a weird coincidence. Right?"

"Probably." Mary took the phone back from Suzie. "But I think it's best to let Jason decide that." She forwarded the photograph to Jason.

"Oh no. He already suspects me. Now he's really going to wonder!" Lizzy shook her head.

"Relax, Lizzy. Snapping a picture doesn't make you a murderer. But it's possible that someone saw the picture you posted, someone that intended to harm Kendra." Suzie grimaced. "There's no way to know right now."

The sound of the front door swinging open drew a gasp from Mary. Pilot launched to his feet and began barking as he ran toward the door.

CHAPTER 6

"Who is that?" Lizzy backed up toward the door that led onto the side of the porch.

"It's okay, Lizzy." Mary slapped her knee. "Pilot, calm down. It's just Wes."

Detective Wes Brown stepped farther into the house. He crouched down and opened his arms to Pilot as he ran toward him with his tail wagging.

"Sorry we startled you." Paul North stepped in behind Wes, and his gaze sought out Suzie.

"It's all right, Paul. Our nerves are just a little rattled." Suzie smiled, then glanced over at Lizzy. "Don't worry, Lizzy. It's just Wes and Paul. Our friends."

"Oh." Lizzy continued to hover near the side door. "You have company. I should go."

"We don't mind if you stay." Paul gestured to one of the chairs at the dining room table. "Please, don't let us run you off."

"No, it's for the best. I need to get home." Lizzy ducked back out the door and hurried across the porch.

"Should I go after her?" Mary stared through the sliding glass doors.

"No, let her go." Suzie turned toward Mary. "This is something she's going to have to work through on her own. If she needs us, I'm sure she'll let us know. We can check in with her later."

Mary turned back to Wes who stood back up as Pilot ran over to Paul.

"Wes, did you come because you heard what happened?" Mary asked.

"Actually, I was already on my way here." Wes gave her a quick kiss. "Paul and I were planning to surprise you by joining in on the yoga class this morning. We were running quite late. We just spoke with Jason and then came here."

"You were going to join us?" Suzie smiled at the thought. "That would have been wonderful."

"It was Paul's idea." Wes put his hands in his

pockets. "I told him you can't teach old dogs new tricks, but he managed to convince me."

"I could have used it." Paul twisted his torso back and forth. "Being on that boat can get a little cramped sometimes." He looked into Suzie's eyes. "Are you doing okay? I'm sure this is not the morning that you expected."

"No, not at all." Suzie looked up at the ceiling. "And certainly not what one of our guests expected on her morning run, either. I think I'll feel better once we figure out what happened to Kendra. Of course, I wish it didn't happen at all, but now that it has, we need to make sure that her killer is caught."

"I met Kendra." Paul glanced toward the sliding glass doors that faced the beach. "I've seen her a few times on the docks with her friends. She's new to town right?"

"Yes. She moved here only about a month or so ago. I had seen her a few times as well, out on the beach. But today, according to her friends, she was alone on the beach. At least, she started out that way," Suzie said.

"Jason will update us as soon as he knows something, I'm sure. But I just can't shake the feeling that whoever did this is still close by." Mary shivered.

"Well, you need to be cautious." Wes put an arm across her shoulders. "I have to work, but I can arrange some security for you."

"No, we don't need security. We'll be fine," Mary said.

"We just need to find the murderer." Suzie's voice grew determined. "Lizzy, who just left, she's the one who found the body. She was supposed to teach the yoga class. She's so shocked. I just want to be able to tell her that she's safe."

"There's a pretty good chance that the killer was only after Kendra." Paul ruffled the fur on Pilot's head. "But I don't like the fact that this happened such a short distance from Dune House, and in daylight. The killer was very bold."

"Or desperate?" Mary suggested. "It looked like whoever did this used the metal detector that Kendra had with her. Maybe it wasn't planned. Maybe the two argued over something, and the killer grabbed whatever was available to use to kill her. That would explain doing it in daylight. It was impulsive."

"It does have the hallmarks of an impulsive murder," Wes said.

"The only problem with that theory is that, according to Kendra's friends, she went out alone on the beach today. So, how did she end up in an argument with someone who wanted to kill her? Maybe she was being followed? Stalked?" Suzie suggested.

"If she was, we know how her stalker might have spotted her." Mary filled them in on the picture that Lizzy had posted as an advertisement. "It came as a complete shock to her that Kendra was in the picture."

"Interesting. I wonder if somehow that picture led the killer to the beach this morning. Do you think it was taken around the same time?" Wes studied the picture.

"In the same place, too. The sun was in the same position as it was in the picture, just like it was this morning when class was due to start. I guess it's possible that the killer suspected Kendra would be out there again this morning," Suzie said.

"Still, it's a bit of a stretch." Paul tilted his head from side to side. "The killer couldn't know for sure that Kendra would be there unless they spoke to her, or followed her."

"If the killer followed her, maybe someone saw them. Jason estimates that the murder took place within an hour of the body being found. One of our guests, Jeanette, was jogging on the beach, and

Lizzy arrived to set up for yoga. We'll have to wait for a more accurate estimate from Summer, but from what I gather, the killer had a very narrow window to commit the crime, because Jeanette and Lizzy didn't see anyone else on the beach," Mary said.

"I wonder if Molly and Michael, our guests who were walking on the beach early this morning, saw anyone. They would have been out there during the estimated time of when the murder took place. Have you told them the news?" Suzie looked over at Mary.

"Oh no. I forgot to tell you." Mary grabbed the note from the reception desk.

"They checked out when we were on the beach."

"They did?" Suzie read the note. "I'll send a text to Jason, so he can contact them."

"Seems strange, doesn't it. Do you think they might be involved in Kendra's murder?" Mary asked.

"If they wanted to disappear after the murder, would they have breakfast here and leave a note?" Suzie raised her eyebrows.

"Maybe. So they wouldn't look suspicious," Paul suggested.

"So, how did the killer follow Kendra, kill her,

and get away with, as far as we know, no one else spotting them?" Suzie looked between them.

"Maybe someone did. I do know of one guy that might have been out there this morning. He likes to go out on his boat fishing in that area early in the morning. Pete. I can check with him to see if he saw anything." Paul looked toward the door. "I'd have to go speak to him in person, though. He doesn't answer his phone."

"Please do." Suzie gave him a quick kiss. "The more information we can get, the better."

"I'm going out fishing for the day soon." Paul glanced at his watch.

"Oh, that's exciting. Your first trip since the fire." Suzie smiled. Paul's boat was damaged in a fire, and although it had been okay for him to live on it, it had taken a while to get it repaired enough, so it could go out on the water.

"I can't wait." Paul rubbed his hands together. "But I'll try to catch up with him before I go. If not, I'll check things out as soon as I get back or first thing in the morning."

"I'll check in on the investigation. My badge should allow me to get any details we might be missing, plus Jason always seems to appreciate my insight." Wes raised his eyebrows as he grinned. "At least that's what I tell myself."

"I'm sure he does." Mary walked with him to the door. "But be careful. Whoever did this isn't going to want to be caught."

"The same goes for you, Mary." Wes looked straight into her eyes. "I know that you want to get to the truth, but please watch your step."

"I will. I promise." Mary waved to him as he left the house with Paul a few steps behind him.

"I think we need to find out more about Kendra." Suzie stepped up beside her. "Without knowing who she was, we're not going to be able to figure out who might have wanted her dead."

"To the library?" Mary smiled.

"Absolutely." Suzie grabbed her purse. "Louis is always the best source of information."

CHAPTER 7

Mary held the door open for Suzie as she stepped into the library. She glanced around the nearly empty space. Her gaze settled on the librarian seated behind his desk.

"Louis." Mary walked toward him.

"I guess you heard what happened to Kendra?" Louis looked up and adjusted his wire-rimmed glasses.

"Yes, we know what happened." Suzie stepped up to the desk beside Mary. "Did you know her well?"

"Not exactly. I just hired her last week. She was supposed to start this afternoon. It's just such a shock to think that someone I just hired has been killed. She was so young. Only in her thirties."

Louis gestured to the chair in front of him. "Just last week she sat in this chair across from me and told me how much she would love to work with me. When I told her she had the job, she was so excited. I felt as if I'd made a big difference in her life. I was really looking forward to working with her, and getting to know her."

"I'm so sorry, Louis." Suzie softened her voice. "The news must have been very hard to hear."

"Yes, it was." Louis met her eyes. "Especially since I heard it from Marty, the newspaper delivery guy. He dropped off the bundle and mentioned it as if it was the juiciest tidbit he could share with me. I swear, he might as well have been salivating. He wanted to know every detail I knew about her. But I didn't share anything. I have no interest in gossiping about her. A murder victim. At least not with him. And now, not to be cold, but I really have to find someone to fill her spot. I needed the help as soon as possible, and obviously she can't offer that now. I'm doing research for a project on rare books, so I need some help here to free up a bit of time." He leaned forward. "I hate to replace Kendra. That just feels wrong to do, but it has to be done."

"This must be very hard for you. Is there any

way that we can help?" Mary reached across the desk and squeezed his shoulder.

"No, it's okay. Thank you. Luckily, I have someone to fill the position. I would have hired her if Kendra hadn't applied." Louis pointed at the phone. "I just left a message to let Leanne know the job is hers."

"Leanne? Kendra's friend, Leanne?" Suzie's voice tightened.

"Yes, her friend. I had intended to give the job to Leanne. She's a local. She's lived here all her life. I thought that would lend her some special insight to offer to the patrons of the library. But Kendra was more qualified when it came to computer literacy. She also had some great ideas for children's programs and even offered to teach a class on metal detecting." Louis smiled some. "She was quite passionate about treasure hunting."

"We believe that she was likely doing just that when she was killed. To think she had gone out there excited to find something great," Mary said.

"She'd made some amazing finds over the years, that's for sure. She told me about a few of them." Louis lowered his voice as he leaned close to them. "I didn't believe everything she said. Some seemed like tall tales. But to me, if you can find something that you enjoy spending your time doing, then you are a very lucky person."

"That's true. But it's possible they weren't tales. Something led to her being killed on that beach," Mary said.

"Do you think she found something that might have gotten her killed?" Louis' eyes widened. "That's intriguing. What if she discovered some kind of ancient artifact?"

"It's more likely she just crossed the wrong person." Suzie looked at Louis. "You said you gave her the job over Leanne? They were supposed to be friends. Maybe Leanne didn't take that very well."

"You suspect Leanne?" Louis sat back in his chair and looked up at the ceiling. "I've known her for a long time." He shook his head as he looked back at them both. "I can't recall a single time that she's done anything that made me think she'd cause anyone harm."

"Do you know her well?" Mary looked into his eyes. "Personally? What her life is like? Has she struggled? Does she have a family?"

"Not much family, no. She's an only child. Her parents are deceased. She never had any children, and she divorced from her high-school sweetheart about two or three years ago." Louis tapped a few keys on his keyboard. "I made some notes on her application about a few things that stood out to me during our interview." He nodded as he looked away from the monitor. "Yes, I was a little concerned that she seemed so anxious to have the job. You know it doesn't pay very well, and she seemed to really be in need of a steady income. I was a little concerned that she would only keep the job long enough to find something better, as she'd need more money than the library can offer."

"Did she say she was having some financial troubles?" Suzie asked.

"She didn't really say it as much as she showed it. She asked about the pay right away, and when she would be able to start. She even asked if she might be able to work extra hours for some overtime. I told her there's not really much opportunity for overtime here." Louis pushed himself back from his desk and stood up from his chair. "But please don't take anything I say as fact. I just assumed a lot from her body language, and I perceived some desperation in the way she talked to me. That doesn't mean I'm right. I wouldn't want to get her into any trouble just because I happened to be a bit critical that day."

"Of course not, Louis. We know that you would

never want that. But this information is actually really important. If Leanne really is in some kind of financial trouble, she might have had a strong reaction to Kendra getting the job. When Kendra came in for the interview did she mention that she and Leanne were friends?" Mary pursed her lips. "I'm a little surprised that she would even apply if she knew that Leanne wanted the job."

"She mentioned that Leanne had told her about the job. But I knew they were friends already. Their group meets here sometimes to discuss finds or plan out days and places to search." Louis picked up a piece of paper and held it out to Suzie. "They even started advertising."

"They were recruiting more people for their club?" Suzie looked over the paper. "Spend time together and find priceless friendship and priceless treasure?" She looked up at Louis. "Did you notice anyone expressing interest in joining?"

"Not yet, no. But they had only just decided to start actively seeking new members. Actually, Kendra had called me and asked me to hold off on handing out the flyers. That's why they're still on my desk." Louis pointed at them.

"Did she say why she wanted you to hold off?" Mary peered at the paper, then looked up at him.

"No, not really. I warned her that it would cost a lot to redo the flyers if she intended to change anything. She said that wasn't the problem, but to just wait to hand them out. I didn't think much of it. The whole group tended to be pretty argumentative. I'd have to go over and ask them to quiet down a few times during their meetings." Louis looked between them. "I'm sorry, I wish I had more to share with you. But that's all I know."

"Thanks, Louis. You've been a lot of help." Mary squeezed his shoulder again. "Let me know if you need to talk, or anything at all."

"Thanks, I will." Louis paused as he looked into her eyes. "And do let me know if you find out what happened. I still can't believe she's gone."

CHAPTER 8

"It sounds to me like we need to speak to Leanne. She didn't say a word about Kendra taking a job from her when Jason spoke to her this morning." Suzie led the way toward the car.

"No, but I'm not sure that's suspicious. Why would she volunteer information like that?" Mary settled in the passenger seat as Suzie started the engine. "But it might explain why Kendra was searching for treasure alone this morning. I'd suspect that Leanne didn't have any interest in spending time with her after that happened."

"Or, she did agree to go with her, and decided to get some revenge." Suzie used her phone to look up Leanne's address. "We won't know anything at all until we go speak with her."

"I'll send an update to Jason just in case he hasn't come across this information." Mary pulled her phone out of her purse and began typing out a text.

"It seems odd to me that of her three friends, none of them went out with her this morning to search the beach. It just feels off." Suzie turned off the main road onto a side road, then took a left. "This should be the street. Look for number twelve."

"I do think we need to tread lightly. She did just lose her friend." Mary looked out through the side window as the house came into view. "There it is, the green one on the right. It does seem a little odd that they were competing for the same job, but that doesn't mean that she killed her over it. That's such a huge leap to make."

"True, but it doesn't mean that she didn't." Suzie parked in front of the house and looked toward the two cars in the driveway. "It looks like someone is home. I promise, I'll be gentle." She glanced over at Mary, then stepped out of the car. As she made her way up the driveway, she overheard loud voices through the open front door of the house.

"You're lying to me, Will! I know you are!" Leanne's voice grew even louder. "Just be honest!"

"You're crazy, Leanne!" Will's voice rivaled hers in volume. "How dare you even suggest that?" He burst through the doorway and pushed past Suzie, then dodged Mary who had reached the top of the driveway.

"Will, are you okay?" Mary turned toward him as he hurried toward one of the cars in the driveway.

"I don't have anything to say to anyone! Just leave me alone!" Will jerked the driver's side door open and slid inside. He slammed the door shut and started the car at the same time.

"He's fine, just let him go," Leanne called out from the doorway. "He just needs to get it out of his system."

"Get what out of his system? What was all of that about?" Suzie looked straight into her eyes. "It's clear that he was upset, and you are, too."

"Of course we're upset. Our friend died this morning." Leanne crossed her arms as she stared back at Suzie. "Or do you not remember that part?"

"Oh, we remember that part." Mary took a step forward. "We also know that you didn't say a word to the police about you and Kendra having a problem between you."

"A problem?" Leanne looked over at her as her cheeks reddened. "What are you talking about?"

"You might not know, yet, since you were busy arguing with Will, but you should have received a message from the library." Suzie smiled. "Congratulations, Leanne. You got the job."

"Oh, that?" Leanne offered a nervous laugh. "That was nothing. It didn't cause any problems between us."

"No?" Mary narrowed her eyes. "I think it would bother me if I had applied for a job, and my friend was hired instead. How did she know about the job?"

"She didn't. At least, not until I told her about it. I was nervous about my interview, and I discussed it with her. She acted very supportive, and then I found out a couple of days later that she had gone in and applied." Leanne cleared her throat.

"And that she'd been hired?" Suzie searched her eyes. "Didn't that upset you?"

"Sure, it did. It surprised me at first. I asked her why she didn't tell me about it. She claimed that she didn't think it would even come up because she doubted that she would get the job. But she also insisted that it wasn't her fault that I blew my interview." Leanne pursed her lips. "And I suppose it wasn't."

"So, you just forgave her?" Mary asked incredulously. "That's very gracious of you."

"Not exactly. I felt resentful. I just didn't understand why she had to go after the job that I needed. She knew I was having trouble making ends meet, and she never seemed to have that problem. Not only that, but she'd found real treasure while on a hunt just over a week ago. I knew she didn't need the money." Leanne crossed her arms. "So yes, I was a little bitter. But I know better than to let my hard feelings ruin a friendship. She got the job. I didn't. I guess she must have been a better option."

"Treasure?" Suzie stepped closer to her, almost into the doorway. "What kind of treasure?"

"A gold bracelet with diamonds. It looked very expensive. Larry, who knows a lot about jewelry, said it was real, and it would be worth a lot." Leanne smiled. "We were all so excited about it."

"She found a bracelet on the beach?" Mary chuckled. "I never find anything other than mushy seaweed."

"It was just a stroke of luck. It must have washed up from some wreckage, or maybe someone dropped it on the beach, somehow. I'm not sure where it came from. But she found it, and it was probably the best find we've ever had in all the time that we've been hunting." Leanne's eyes lit up with excitement. "It really made us all believe that it might happen again."

"I'm surprised that a find like that wouldn't have made the news, or at least the local gossip." Suzie crossed her arms. "But I didn't hear anything about it."

"She wanted to keep it quiet. She wanted to have the bracelet appraised and decide what she would do with it from there. Of course that caused some controversy in our group." Leanne lowered her voice. "She refused to follow our rules."

"Rules?" Mary met her eyes. "What kind of rules?"

"We usually work in pairs or more. It's more fun that way. But that means that when one of us finds something, there's usually at least another person there. So, we made a rule that if you're together when you find something, then it belongs to everyone that was with you. Kendra was with Will when she found the bracelet. But she insisted that he was several feet away searching another area. She felt that meant it was her find alone. Will disagreed. But she didn't care. It's not like we could do anything to enforce the rule. She wouldn't share the find with Will. To make matters worse, she began wearing the bracelet. She always had it on. Will felt like she was flaunting it." Leanne grimaced. "Look, it's not as if I'm saying that Will had anything to do with this. But when the police showed us the picture of Kendra to identify her, I noticed right away that the bracelet was missing. So, when Will stopped by just before, I asked him if he knew where it was. If he had taken it." She bit into her bottom lip. "I know it's a horrible accusation to make, but I had to know."

"And?" Suzie searched her eyes. "Did he admit to taking it?"

"No. He insisted that he had no idea where it was." Leanne rubbed her hand across her eyes. "I lost one friend today, and I think now I may have lost another."

As Mary witnessed the pain in Leanne's eyes, she believed her. She felt sympathy for her. She'd been caught in the middle of a tumultuous friendship, and now that her friend had been killed, she still had to navigate the hurt feelings that carried on even after her death.

"Emotions are high right now, Leanne. I'm sure that Will knows you care about him."

"I do. I was only trying to look out for him. If he did take that bracelet, can you imagine how that would look to the police?" Leanne's eyes widened. "They'd probably think that Will killed her."

CHAPTER 9

"And you don't think it's possible that Will killed her?" Suzie slid her hands into her pockets as she studied Leanne's expression to see if it gave anything away. "You said yourself you think he might have taken the bracelet."

"Taken the bracelet, yes, to prevent it from falling into someone else's hands or disappearing. He would never have killed her to take it. Are you crazy?" Leanne clucked her tongue. "Absolutely not. Will is a good man. He's a fair man. When Kendra refused to share the money from the bracelet with him, he could have quit the group, he could have harassed her, or made it a huge issue. Instead, he let it go because that's the kind of man he is. You have no right to stand here and accuse my friend of doing such a terrible thing."

"We're not accusing him of anything." Mary attempted to reassure her as her heart began to race. "Please, Leanne, we know that you've been through a lot. We didn't mean to upset you."

"Yes, I've been through a lot. My friend has been killed, and you think that it's a good idea to accuse my other friend of killing her?" Leanne gasped as she looked into Mary's eyes. "Is that why you asked about Kendra's job? Because you think I would have killed her so I could get the job?"

"No, we're just trying to work out what was happening in her life." Suzie held up her hands.

"Look, I have to go." Leanne closed the door.

"We need to find out more from Will, and more about this bracelet." Mary turned toward Suzie.

"You're absolutely right." Suzie led the way back to the car. "I'm going to text Jason about this." She pulled out her phone. "I think we also need to consider that there could be a new motive."

"What's that?" Mary climbed into the car.

Suzie started the engine, then looked over at her.

"Robbery. If Kendra really was parading around wearing a rare diamond bracelet worth who knows how much, maybe someone spotted her and decided they wanted the bracelet for themselves. She went out onto that beach all alone, and if she was wearing that bracelet, she wasn't wearing it when her body was found. Which means there's a good chance that someone killed her and took it off her."

"Leanne said she would never take it off." Mary chewed on her bottom lip as she considered it. "So, maybe someone spotted her with the bracelet and followed her around until they saw her alone, then just attacked."

"I think it's possible. The key here is that we need to find out if she had that bracelet on when she stepped onto the beach this morning. If anyone had a motive to steal that bracelet from her, it's definitely Will." Suzie turned down another street. "He lives only a few minutes from here."

"I'm not sure that he's going to be in the mood to speak with us after the way he left Leanne's house."

"Maybe not, but we can give it a try. We need to speak to him while everything is still fresh, and he's still emotional. He might panic and make a mistake that can tell us whether or not he was involved." Suzie turned onto another road. "His house is on the corner."

"Leanne seemed to think he would never hurt Kendra. They're friends. Maybe she's right."

"Maybe. But people can do some very unexpected things when they're under pressure. And we don't always know people as well as we think."

"Heads up, Suzie. He's outside." Mary looked toward the house.

"It looks like he's on his way out of town." Suzie slowed to a stop in front of Will's driveway. He was carrying a large suitcase. "I'll just make sure he can't back out of here and take off."

"Do you think that's a good idea?" Mary sat up straighter. "If he's really in a panic, he might just ram your car."

"Let him try. It will at least slow him down. He's not getting anywhere without me talking to him first. He might be the murderer and doing a runner." Suzie popped open the door of the car and stepped out. "Will?"

"I don't have time to talk right now." Will refused to look in her direction as he loaded the suitcase into the trunk. "Please move your car!"

"In a minute." Suzie crossed her arms as Mary stepped out of the car as well. "I need to speak with you, Will, about Kendra."

"I don't have anything to say about it." Will finally turned to face the two women. "I wasn't there, I don't know what happened to her, and I don't want to talk about it."

"I understand. You must be grieving." Mary edged her way closer to him. "But you have to understand that as Kendra's friend, you might have very important information about what led to her tragic death. That must be important to you, right?"

"We weren't friends." Will glared at Mary. "I'm sure that Leanne told you that much."

"We want to hear it from you. Not anyone else." Suzie settled her gaze on him. "Do you really want someone else speaking for you?"

"No." Will's tone sharpened. "No one else can. Listen, if I thought I could do anything to help, I would. But I don't know anything. We hadn't known each other very long, and the only thing we had in common was looking for treasure. That was it. I like to keep to myself. I don't want to get into the middle of people's business. What happened to Kendra is exactly why."

"Do you think she was involved with something that got her killed?" Suzie searched his expression for any slight changes to indicate if he was hiding something. "Did she mention something to you about that?"

"No. I don't have a clue what got her killed. I've

already said that, so don't try to twist my words." Will scowled as he opened the door to his car. "Now, move your car before I move it for you."

"Will, you have to understand that leaving town is going to lead people to make assumptions about you. Including the police." Suzie stepped in front of his car. "You're better off sticking around and being helpful than asking to be a suspect."

"What?" Will glared at her. "I'm not a suspect. I had nothing to do with Kendra dying."

Mary cleared her throat as Jason's car pulled to a stop right behind Suzie's.

"It looks like you missed your chance, Will."

"Great!" Will snarled as he slammed the car door shut. "Now, I have to deal with this guy."

CHAPTER 10

Suzie took a step back as Jason approached Will.

Jason shot a quick glance at her, and then at Mary, before focusing his attention on Will.

"Going somewhere?" Jason rested his hands on his belt as he looked over the boxes and suitcases in the back of Will's car.

"I was trying to, but these two illegally blocked my driveway and held me hostage." Will glared at Suzie and Mary. "Are you going to do something about this?" He turned toward Jason. "Or are you just going to stand by and let them harass me, intimidate me, when I've done nothing wrong?"

"Well now, I happen to know that they don't have a history of being very intimidating." Jason looked over at them, then shifted his gaze back to Will. "But you do have a history with my murder victim, and it sure looks like you're wanting to leave town."

"I'm free to do whatever I want." Will held up his hands. "Right? I know you're not here to arrest me, because I had nothing to do with Kendra's death. So, as far as I'm concerned, it's none of your business what my plans are or where I'm going."

"You're wrong about that." Jason's tone hardened, but he continued to maintain his distance. "As of now, everyone in that metal-detecting group is a suspect. As far as I know you were her only friends in this town. I need your information and insight to help me with this investigation. So, I'm requesting that you don't leave town until I'm able to gather all of the information I need. Right now it's a request. If you want me to go further than that, it's going to get legal and messy. So, can we just agree to you sticking around until all of this is sorted out?"

"Agree?" Will glared at Jason. "How can I agree to anything when you're basically threatening me? You're saying do what you tell me to do or you're going to make my life even harder. So no, I don't agree. But it seems I don't have a choice, either." He took a step away from his car. "I don't have the means to fight a legal battle when the police have an agenda. I don't care what anyone told you about me. You know me. You know I would never hurt someone. I would certainly never kill anyone. Especially one of my friends."

"But you did just tell us that you and Kendra weren't friends." Suzie tightened her lips as she watched Will's reaction to her words.

He groaned in frustration and curled his hands into fists at his sides.

"See? I knew you would twist my words and try to use them against me. This is ridiculous. I had nothing to do with this! Why am I the one being treated like a criminal?" Will stomped one foot against the driveway. "Get out of here! Get off my property!"

"Why are you so angry?" Jason crossed his arms. He didn't move an inch back from Will. His muscles tensed as he watched the man closely. "I just asked you to help me figure out who killed your friend."

"I just know you're going to try pin this on me." Will frowned.

"Is it because of the bracelet, Will? The bracelet that has gone missing. Do you have it packed in one of those boxes in your car? Were you going to use it to fund your getaway?" Mary tried to sound more confident than she felt.

Suzie caught Mary's arm at the same moment that Jason moved to stand between Will and Mary, offering her some protection from the furious scowl that Will leveled on her.

"I think we need to have a conversation, Will. Alone?" Jason cast a heavy glance from Mary to Suzie.

"I didn't take that stupid bracelet!" Will shouted. "Even if I did, it wouldn't be stealing! It belonged to me! She never should have kept it for herself! I did nothing wrong!"

"All right, all right." Jason held up his hands and softened his tone. "I'm not saying that you stole anything. What I'm saying is that I'd like to talk with you about it. Can we do that? Can we just have a conversation?"

"You're not putting any handcuffs on me." Will glared at him. "These two are my witnesses if you do anything to hurt me."

"I won't." Jason took a step toward him with his hands still raised in the air. "All I'm asking for is your help. I'm not trying to cause you any trouble. But right now, I need to understand everything I can about Kendra's life, and that includes where that bracelet might have gone. You say you don't have it." He lowered his hands. "Well then, I believe you. But that leaves us with another mystery to solve. The bracelet could be the clue that leads me to Kendra's killer. So, if you share as much as you can with me about it, this whole thing might be solved before any of us sit down for dinner tonight. Does that sound good?"

"Sure, I guess. If you just want some information, I can give you that. But I don't know much." Will put his hands in his pockets.

"That's fine. Anything you can tell me might be helpful." Jason gestured toward the house. "Why don't we go inside to discuss it? I'm sure you'd prefer some privacy. Right?"

"Yes, I would. I don't need the neighbors gossiping about me being involved in a murder." Will turned toward the house. "But don't think I won't record every single minute of our conversation. You're not going to trick me into saying anything that you can use to make up a story to use against me."

"Don't worry, Will. Like I said, it's just a conversation." Jason glanced over his shoulder at Suzie and Mary, then followed Will toward the door of his house.

"I guess we're not going to be privy to that conversation." Mary watched the door swing shut.

"No, but at least he isn't driving off into the sunset. Jason will make him stick around." Suzie walked back over to the car and opened the driver's side door. "And while he's busy talking to Will, he won't notice if you and I pay Summer a visit."

"Are you sure about that?" Mary climbed into the passenger seat. "Jason doesn't miss a lot, and Summer is his wife. She'll probably let him know that we were there."

"Probably, but by the time he's finished with Will, we might find out something important. We can at least try, can't we?" Suzie flashed Mary a smile as she started the car. "We need to try and find out if Kendra was wearing that bracelet when she was killed. If she did wear it to the beach this morning, that means that whoever killed her likely took it."

"True." Mary stared out the window as the car rolled closer to town. "Do you think Will might have done it? He felt slighted by Kendra not sharing the find with him."

"Maybe. The way he was acting just now, as angry as he seemed to get, I think it's possible. At this point, we can't really rule anyone out." Suzie turned into the parking lot of the medical examiner's office and parked near the entrance. As she turned off the car, she looked over at Mary. "What really surprises me is that she found this valuable bracelet, then she proceeded to wear it. Who does that? If you found something worth a lot of money, would you just wear it? Or would you put it somewhere safe?"

"It's an odd decision. You're right. But maybe she just wanted to show off her find." Mary stepped out of the car. "She certainly made herself a target, one way or another."

"Maybe Summer has turned up something that will give us more insight." Suzie held the front door open for Mary.

"Let's just hope she's in the mood to share it with us."

CHAPTER 11

Suzie and Mary walked into the medical examiner's office.

"Hi, Suzie, Mary." Dwayne turned around to face them from behind the front desk.

"Hi, Dwayne. We just wanted to have a quick conversation with Summer if she's free, please?" Mary smiled at the young receptionist.

"I'll check." Dwayne picked up his phone and mumbled a few words into it. "She said you can go on back. Give her a second and she'll meet you in the hallway."

Mary cringed inwardly. She preferred not to go anywhere near the back of the medical examiner's office.

"Thanks." Suzie started down the hallway.

As Suzie and Mary reached the examination room, Summer walked out through the double doors.

"Sorry, I hope we didn't interrupt," Mary said.

"No, it's fine. I needed a little break." Summer looked between them. "I know you probably want information, but I can't share anything."

"Oh, that's okay. No harm in trying, right." Suzie gave a short laugh.

"Can we get you something to eat? I know you must be so busy." Mary clasped her hands together.

"No, that's okay." Summer hesitated, then continued. "Actually, that would be great."

"Your usual?" Mary asked.

"Yes, please." Summer nodded.

"No problem." Mary turned toward the door. "We'll be right back."

Mary led the way down the hallway with Suzie close behind.

"Dwayne, we're going to the bakery. Can we get you anything?" Mary looked over at him as they headed toward the front door.

"No, but thank you." Dwayne smiled with appreciation. "I'm going on my afternoon break soon."

"Okay." Mary followed Suzie out of the

building. "Well, it doesn't look like Summer is going to tell us anything."

"No. I guess not." Suzie's phone beeped. She looked at the text. "Oh, it looks like the couple that were checking in tonight have canceled."

"They probably heard about the murder." Mary sighed.

"I imagine so. Hopefully, the murderer is found, and this all blows over soon."

"I'm sure it will. Do you want anything? A cupcake?" Mary opened the door to the bakery. "We've barely eaten. We skipped lunch."

"Yes, that sounds good." Suzie's stomach rumbled at the thought.

Mary placed an order for Summer's roast chicken sandwich, three vanilla cupcakes, and three coffees.

After they picked up their order, they stepped out of the bakery. As they did, they noticed Larry and Sheila, Larry's wife, walking down the sidewalk toward the bakery. Suzie and Mary knew Sheila from the diner where she worked as a waitress.

"Afternoon." Sheila smiled at Suzie and Mary.

"Sheila, Larry. How are you?" Suzie smiled slightly at them as she noticed the strain in Larry's expression.

"Still in shock. It's terrible what happened. I just can't believe I wasn't there." Larry looked at the ground. "I just wish I could have protected her."

"We all do." Sheila nodded.

"She was really starting to settle into the group." Larry glanced up at them. "We were all becoming quite good friends. I just can't believe she's gone."

"So everything was okay between the members of the group and Kendra? We heard there was some tension." Mary balanced the coffee tray in her hand.

"Yes, a bit. Between Will and Kendra, but it would have all worked out." Larry shrugged. "People get over things like that."

"And you didn't notice anything this morning as you walked to the beach?" Suzie asked.

"No nothing." Larry glanced at his wife. "I was at home working when I heard from Leanne that the police were on the beach. So, I hurried down there. I had no idea what had happened. I just wanted the gossip really."

"That's all he can tell you." Sheila grabbed Larry's hand and turned toward the bakery. "We have to get going, and it looks like your coffee is getting cold." She opened the bakery door.

"Well, he didn't have much to offer." Mary

glanced over at Suzie as they started toward the medical examiner's office.

"No, he just seemed to brush the tensions in the group off as if they meant nothing." Suzie opened the door for Mary. "And it seemed like Sheila couldn't wait to get him out of the conversation."

"You can go on back. Summer is expecting you." Dwayne passed them in the doorway. "I'm heading out now."

"Thanks." Suzie led the way toward the examination area. "I don't hear the music she usually plays when she's working." Before she could call for Summer, she heard her voice coming from inside the room.

Suzie glanced over at Mary and held her finger to her lips. It sounded like Summer was talking with Jason on speakerphone.

Suzie met Mary's eyes as they started to listen.

"So, what do you have?" Jason asked.

"Not much. She doesn't have any scratches, or bruises. No DNA under her nails. Nothing to indicate what happened," Summer explained.

"The killer tossed the metal detector into the water, and the techs aren't having any luck retrieving evidence from it. But they're going to go through it again in case they missed anything. What about the time of death?"

"The estimate remains the same at the moment. Within an hour of her body being discovered." Summer paused, then continued. "She was killed by numerous blows to the back of her head. I haven't found evidence of water in her lungs, which indicates to me that she was dead before she hit the water."

"So, the nature of the attack would suggest that this was a crime of passion and she knew her killer. And that she might have felt comfortable enough to turn her back to them. It's possible she didn't hear the person coming, so she didn't have a chance to turn around. Or she felt trapped, and she tried to get away by turning toward the water."

"Yes, this definitely looks personal to me."

"She fell into the water on the edge. It looked like she didn't try to run. She just collapsed right at the edge, as if she'd just decided to casually dip her toes in."

"It looks like she didn't see it coming at all," Summer said.

"You didn't by any chance find a bracelet anywhere hidden on her person, did you?" Jason asked.

"No, I didn't find any bracelet. But there's irritation on her wrist, as if she'd recently been wearing one."

Suzie and Mary met each other's gaze. Suzie knew they shouldn't eavesdrop, but she couldn't bring herself to walk away. She really wanted to see if she could find anything out. It was her curious nature and from years of working as an investigative journalist.

"Interesting. I found out that she had recently found an expensive bracelet. She wore it all the time. But it's missing today," Jason said.

"A bracelet. Maybe a stranger just wanted to steal it?"

"Maybe, but I still think this was a crime of passion, and it's more likely she was familiar with her murderer. She wasn't very open with her friends. I get the feeling that she had a lot to hide."

"Did you check out the tattoo?" Summer asked.

"Yes. I did a quick search and couldn't match it." The sound of Jason paging through his notes came over the speakerphone. "I'll keep looking. It's probably a custom design."

"Interesting. Maybe if you can find out what it stands for, it will lead us to more information about her," Summer said.

"I'll do another search. Do you have any idea how tall the killer would have been, from the angle of the blows?" Jason asked.

"Not much taller than Kendra. I wish I had something more definitive. I know it's not much to go on."

"It's a place to start."

"I'll send through a preliminary report soon."

"Thanks. I'll call you after I've gone through it." Jason ended the call.

Suzie glanced over at Mary and waited a few seconds.

"Summer," Suzie called out as if they had just arrived.

"Suzie, hold on a second. I'll be right out." After a couple of minutes, Summer pushed open the double doors. "Oh, thank you so much." She took the sandwich from Mary as the phone in her office rang. "Sorry, Dwayne isn't here, so I better check who it is."

"No problem. A cupcake and coffee as well." Suzie placed them on the bench in front of her, and Summer's eyes lit up in appreciation.

"Thank you."

"Anytime." Mary smiled. "We'll catch up later."

Suzie and Mary headed toward the front door as Summer turned toward her office.

"Well, we learned a lot, didn't we?" Suzie walked with Mary toward her car.

"We certainly did."

"We know that Kendra most likely knew her murderer. It doesn't sound like a random attack." Suzie glanced over at Mary.

"Do you really think someone she was friends with could have done this?"

"Honestly, Mary, I'm starting to think that she didn't really have any close friends, or anyone that knew her very well."

"I'm having a hard time believing that someone could be killed so close to Dune House without anyone seeing or hearing anything. I just hope we can figure out who did this."

Suzie's phone beeped with a text. She slipped it out of her purse and looked at it.

"It's from Jason. He wants us to go down to the station to discuss something with him."

"Discuss?" Mary had a sip of coffee. "Is this going to be the 'stay out of police business' lecture?"

"It might be." Suzie slid her phone back into her purse. "Only one way to find out."

CHAPTER 12

Mary stared at the entrance to the police station as Suzie parked. She hesitated, while Suzie unbuckled her seat belt and began to step out of the car.

"Mary? Are you coming?" She stuck her head back through the door.

"I'm not sure I want to." Mary continued to stare through the windshield. "How upset do you think he'll be that we've been investigating on our own?"

"Oh, I think Jason is used to us by now. I wouldn't worry about it too much." Suzie waved her hand through the air. "Besides, he's all bark and no bite."

"Sure, it's easy for you to say that. He's more

forgiving that you stick your nose into these things, because you were an investigative reporter and you're his cousin." Mary reluctantly stepped out of the car. "He doesn't think the same about me. He thinks I have no place doing a little snooping."

"Mary, you know that's not true." Suzie stopped on the sidewalk in front of the police station to wait for her. "Jason loves you like family, the same way he loves me."

"Jason is waiting for you." An officer looked up at them from behind the front desk. "He's down the hall in the conference room."

"Thank you." Suzie smiled, then led the way.

"Suzie, Mary." Jason's voice summoned them farther down the hall. He held open the door to the conference room. "Thanks for coming by." He waved them inside. "We've set up in here. I'm hoping that getting as many heads together on this as possible will lead to finding our suspect quickly." He let the door fall closed behind them. "Beth is helping me sort through some financial records at the moment. I appreciate you telling me about the bracelet. Leanne and Will didn't mention it to me when I first spoke to them." He gestured for them to take a seat around the large table in the middle of the room. "As of now, we haven't been able to find it. We combed through the items she had with her, also her house, and her car, which was parked at the beach." He looked over the paperwork on the table. "So far, nothing. But we're still looking for any alternative storage we might have missed."

"Leanne insisted that Kendra always had the bracelet on, that's why she noticed right away that it was missing." Mary sat down in one of the chairs.

"And Summer said there was some irritation around her wrist, indicating she recently had a bracelet on," Jason said.

"Which means you can't rule out the possibility that she had it on when she was murdered." Suzie pulled out a chair beside Mary and sat down. "What did Will have to say about it?"

"Unfortunately, not much. He doesn't trust the police in general, so getting him to speak to me at all was a bit of a struggle. He insisted that he has no idea where the bracelet is, or who killed Kendra," Jason said.

"Do you believe him?" Suzie looked into his eyes.

"I'm not sure what to believe just yet. The only thing I do know for sure is that Kendra is a mystery." Jason gestured to some files spread out on the table. "I can't find any history of her before she moved to Garber. I've been digging into her past, and I keep hitting dead ends. She has no employment history that I can find, barely any money in the bank. But she bought her house and car outright, and she seems to live a very comfortable lifestyle."

"Gobs of money and a missing past usually indicates some kind of criminal activity." Beth plopped down into a chair on the other side of the table. "I think maybe she was on the run, and her past caught up with her."

"Is that Kendra's tattoo?" Suzie pointed to a picture on the table in front of Jason. It was on the back of a shoulder. It was of a dragon breathing fire.

"Ah yes, the tattoo." Jason looked at it. "So far I haven't turned up much about it, but I'm going to keep looking. It could just be a tattoo she got on a whim. Summer said it definitely wasn't recent. It was at least a few years old." He looked down at the pile of paperwork in front of him. "I'm starting to wonder if she changed her name. That would explain why I can't find any past records on her. Her fingerprints aren't on record."

"Hmm, if she changed her name, then she probably really was on the run from someone or something." Mary looked over his desk. "She didn't seem to want to share much about her life even with her metal-detecting friends."

"Yes, everyone I've spoken to about her indicated she was a pretty private person." Jason looked between them.

"She led a secretive life, which means it might take a lot of effort to get to the truth," Mary said.

"Paul is going to check with his fishermen friends to see if anyone saw anything unusual on the beach this morning. I haven't heard back from him, yet. He had to go out fishing. I'll let you know if he finds anything." Suzie tapped her fingers against the table.

"Great." Jason looked over at her.

"Were there any other witnesses?" Suzie asked.

"As of now, the only four people I know were on the beach during the estimated window of when the murder took place are Lizzy, and your guests, Michael, Molly, and Jeanette. I'll keep trying, but I haven't been able to contact Michael or Molly," Jason said.

"That's strange." Mary narrowed her eyes. "They were so quick to leave this morning."

"We just saw Larry in town with his wife. She didn't seem to want Larry to talk about Kendra and the group," Suzie said.

"Well, Larry has been very cooperative, answered all my questions, but he didn't have much to offer." Jason looked up at them. "I also spoke to your other guest Josh, and he didn't leave Dune House until long after the body was found."

"Yes, he only came downstairs after Lizzy, Jeanette, and I had returned to Dune House." Mary nodded.

"Lizzy is new in town, too, right?" Beth looked up at him. "Maybe there's a connection there?"

"Maybe. But right now we're just grasping at straws. We need something concrete to get this investigation going in the right direction. That's why I asked you two to come in." Jason shifted his gaze back to them. "I need your help."

"Sure, anything you need." Suzie leaned forward. She was eager to help with the investigation.

"Jeanette's insisting that she already told me everything she knows. But I'm not convinced she has." Jason narrowed his eyes. "Something feels off about the statement she gave me, but I can't put my finger on it. Obviously, I can't ask you to act in any official capacity, but she might be more willing to talk to you. I'm concerned that maybe she did see something but is just too scared by what she saw to come forward about it."

"I hadn't thought about that. That's definitely possible. She keeps saying she didn't see anything, but that could be because she's scared. We'll see what we can find out and let you know." Suzie stood up from her chair. "Was there anything else you needed?"

"No, just keep an ear out." Jason met her eyes as Mary stood up as well.

CHAPTER 13

"We need to speak to Jeanette. Jason's hunches are rarely wrong." Suzie led the way to the front door of the police station.

"True, but do you really think Jeanette is hiding something?" Mary stepped out through the door that Suzie held open for her. "What could scare her enough to keep her from wanting to solve a murder?"

"Maybe the killer threatened her? Or maybe she recognized the killer?" Suzie opened the driver's side door to the car. "Maybe just witnessing the murder was enough to terrify her."

"But if she did witness the murder, that would mean she saw Kendra get killed, then ran down the beach. When she came back, she pretended not to know anything about the murder. That's a lot of effort to go to just to avoid admitting she's a witness." Mary settled in the passenger seat. "If she did recognize the killer, then maybe she wants to protect them? Maybe it's someone she knows?"

"Only one way to find out. We have to ask her more questions." Suzie turned out of the parking lot and headed in the direction of Dune House. "But I think if we gang up on her she's going to shut down. Maybe it would be best if you talk to her."

"Me?" Mary glanced over at her. "Why me? You're much better at asking questions."

"I might be better at interrogating people, but that's not what we want to do here. You have a way with people, Mary. You put them at ease. I think it's the mother in you." Suzie winked at her. "What do you say? Want to give it a try?"

"Sure, I can try." Mary nodded as Suzie turned the car into the parking lot of Dune House. "But I'm not sure she's going to talk to me."

"It's worth a shot." Suzie parked, then stepped out of the car. "I'm going to let you take the lead, then I'll make some excuse to leave the two of you alone."

"I'll do my best." Mary followed her. "I can offer

her something to eat. I think I'm just going to have an early dinner of sandwiches. I still feel a bit hungry, even after that cupcake, but I don't want anything too heavy. Can I make you something else?"

"No, thank you. Sandwiches would be great."

"I'll make something else for Josh and Jeanette if they want me to."

"Perfect." Suzie opened the door and smiled as she dropped down to her knees to greet Pilot.

Mary spotted Jeanette as she descended the stairs into the living room.

"Hi, Jeanette, I'm going to put together something to eat. An early dinner. We were just going to have sandwiches, but I can also make something more substantial for you later. Is turkey breast and ham okay for you? We have swiss, and cheddar cheese. Would you like both?" Mary rattled off her questions as she continued toward the kitchen. Only when she reached the doorway, did she process the suitcase she'd seen by the front door. "Oh, are you leaving?" She turned around to face Jeanette who hovered near the suitcase.

"Yes, I think that would be best. I took another shower to try to clear my head, and I just feel very strange about staying here. No offense to you or to

Suzie, you've both been wonderful hosts, but a woman has been killed." Jeanette flinched. "It just doesn't feel right to be on vacation after that happened."

"Oh, I do understand." Mary met her eyes. "But I wish you would reconsider. Suzie and I discussed it and already decided to refund your whole stay. You can stay to give you time to process what happened. And you don't want to drive in the dark, do you?" She glanced over at Suzie, who gave a short nod, then looked back at Jeanette. "Even if you still want to leave, please at least eat something, so that you'll be full for your journey."

"That's so kind of you to offer." Jeanette started to reach for her suitcase, then hesitated. "I just don't know what to do, I guess. I never expected something like this to happen."

"It's a long drive home." Suzie gestured to the dining room table. "Why don't you relax and talk with us a little bit? You don't have to decide anything right now."

"Thanks, that does sound nice." Jeanette's voice wavered as she walked toward the table. "And anything you want to put on the sandwich would be fine. I actually am very hungry." She sat down at the table. "I just can't wrap my head around this. Do you know if they have focused in on a suspect, yet? I think that would put me more at ease."

"Unfortunately, not yet." Suzie sat down at the table with Jeanette while Mary headed into the kitchen. "But they're very early on in the investigation at the moment. There are some possible leads."

"The police don't believe this was a random attack," Mary called over her shoulder as she washed her hands. "I know that may not make you feel any safer, but I hope that it does."

"It does, a little," Jeanette said.

"Since you're from out of town, and didn't know Kendra at all, I really don't think the murderer would have any interest in you. And I can assure you that we will do everything we can to make sure that you're safe, if you decide to stay. Pilot is a great watchdog." Suzie smiled as the dog trotted toward the dining room table at the sound of his name. He looked at Jeanette, then at Suzie, and gave a sharp bark.

"He's a little antsy, too, I imagine." Mary carried a tray of sandwiches out to the dining room table. "I hope that the police will be able to make an arrest, quickly, but with so few witnesses on the beach, it may be hard for them to do."

"I wish I had more to offer them. When I run, I have my music blasting. I go into another state of mind and I don't really pay attention to what's around me." Jeanette picked up one of the sandwiches. "Maybe once I eat I'll feel a little better."

"I'm going to take Pilot out." Suzie stood up from the table. "We'll be back shortly." She grabbed Pilot's leash from the hook by the front door and clipped it to his collar.

Jeanette took a bite of her sandwich.

"Jeanette, I know what it's like to get lost in my music. Sometimes, I listen to it while I clean or cook." Mary picked up one of the sandwiches as well. "And it may seem like I don't hear or notice anything when I'm in that zone. But sometimes we notice more than we think."

"You still think I might know something?" Jeanette narrowed her eyes. "I'm sorry, but I don't."

"Do you remember how it felt running on the beach?" Mary sat back in her chair. "Was it cold, or warm?"

"Cold, at first. And the sand was slippery. I was a little worried that I wasn't really prepared for running in the sand. I don't usually run on the beach," Jeanette said.

"It's a lot different, right?" Mary smiled. "I know, for me, even just walking on the beach can be a little tricky."

"Yes. But it was beautiful. After running for a bit, I remember looking out over the water." Jeanette looked toward the sliding glass doors that overlooked the ocean. "It felt like I was the only person that existed."

"And when you looked out over the water, was your music playing?" Mary leaned closer to her.

"No. It was switching between songs. It was so quiet for a moment." Jeanette smiled a little. "I think that's why it felt especially peaceful."

"And did you hear anything right at that moment? Maybe something far away, that you didn't even notice?" Mary asked.

Jeanette's eyes suddenly widened.

"Yes. Yes, now that I'm thinking about it, I actually did hear something."

"What did you hear?" Mary gazed into her eyes.

"Please, no," Jeanette whispered the words as she shivered. "Or maybe, please, don't. I don't remember exactly. It was far away, and with the noise of the waves I didn't really think about it. It didn't sound like someone was in trouble. It sounded more like someone was just talking."

"Do you remember anything about the voice? Was it a man, or a woman speaking?" Mary's heart pounded.

"A woman." Tears filled Jeanette's eyes. "Do you think it was her? Do you think it was Kendra?"

"What was Kendra?" Suzie stepped back through the front door of Dune House just as Jeanette finished her question.

"Jeanette might have heard Kendra." Mary grabbed a tissue from the middle of the table and offered it to Jeanette.

"I guess it could have been her." Jeanette wiped her eyes.

"Where were you on the beach?" Mary asked.

"I don't know exactly, but quite close to where she was found." Jeannette sniffed.

"I thought you said you didn't hear or see anything?" Suzie sat down beside Mary.

Pilot settled his head in her lap.

"Aren't you thirsty, Pilot?" Suzie patted his head. "Go have some water."

Pilot looked up at her but didn't budge.

"I thought I hadn't heard anything. But when I talked with Mary, I remembered a moment that the music stopped." Jeanette shook her head. "I'm sure it doesn't make any difference to the case. I can't even remember exactly what I heard. It's possible that it wasn't even Kendra."

"It might have been, though." Suzie pulled her phone out of her pocket. "Jason will definitely want to hear about this. I can call him if you want?"

"Great. Thank you." Jeanette picked up another sandwich from the plate. "I've told you everything I know." She stood up from her chair. "But I think I will stay another night instead of driving in the dark. But I do want to leave in the morning. At this point, I don't think I'll be able to rest until I know that Kendra's killer has been caught. The thought that I might have heard her last words." She shuddered. "I'll see you in the morning. Thanks for the sandwiches." She hurried across the dining room through the living room. She picked up her suitcase and headed up the stairs that led to the second floor.

"At least she's staying." Suzie watched her go, then picked up a sandwich.

"I can't believe she actually heard something, after all." Mary sat back in her chair. "Too bad it doesn't lead to much."

Pilot lifted his head, sniffed the air, then trotted into the kitchen straight to his water bowl.

"Let me fill that for you." Mary walked after him.

"I sent Jason the information. Maybe he'll be able to use it." Suzie looked at her phone. "Paul texted that he's still out and will be late back, so he'll catch up with me tomorrow."

"Wes is also working late." Mary filled Pilot's water bowl and put it back on the floor.

"I wouldn't mind staying up late to try to talk to Josh, but he often works very late, and then goes out until all hours of the morning, so I think we should leave it until tomorrow."

"I agree. I think we should call it a night and get started early in the morning. There isn't much else we can do now. I want to finish my book. I'm near the end. I want to find out who the murderer is."

"Good idea." Suzie smiled.

"Come on, buddy." Mary gestured for Pilot to follow her. He wagged his tail. Mary often said that she would stop letting Pilot sleep in her bed, but she never did. She loved his company.

CHAPTER 14

"Morning." Suzie walked into the kitchen, and the aroma of apple and cinnamon immediately hit her. "Something smells delicious."

"Apple cinnamon muffins." Mary smiled from beside the oven.

"Oh, yum." Suzie watched as Pilot ran over to greet her. She bent down to kiss Pilot's head, then looked up at Mary. "Did you sleep well?"

"Yes, surprisingly. I fell asleep before I finished the first page. I think I was just so tired from the events of the day." Mary handed her a cup of coffee and pulled the muffins from the oven. "And you?"

"It took me a while to get to sleep but once I

was, I slept soundly." Suzie glanced at the front door as it swung open.

"Paul! Just in time for breakfast." Mary smiled as she looked at him.

"Great, I'm starving." Paul patted his stomach.

"How was the trip?" Suzie walked toward him.

"It was great to be out there again. And I got a good haul." Paul placed a light kiss on Suzie's lips. "I've asked around the docks, and unfortunately I didn't find out much. I was hoping to be able to crack the case for you."

"It's okay." Suzie smiled. "We're going to figure this out."

"I did manage to speak to someone who was out on the water." Paul glanced over at Mary as she carried a cup of coffee toward him. "Oh yes, thank you so much, Mary."

"What did you find out?" Mary pursed her lips. "That coffee isn't free, you know?"

"Is that so?" Paul grinned, then took a sip. "I managed to speak to Pete. He was out fishing on his boat in the area near where Kendra was found. He said that he was alone out there for over an hour from about five, but it was dark for some of the time, and he didn't have a view of the beach the whole time. He didn't see Kendra or anyone else out on the beach. It's not very helpful."

"So, he was probably out there long before her body was found," Suzie said.

"According to him he saw the police cars arriving when he was walking into town, after he had docked and sorted out his haul. So, I'd guess he finished at least an hour before Kendra's body was discovered. He didn't give me an exact time of when he finished, though." Paul took another sip of his coffee.

"If he saw the police, did he stop to see what was happening? Did he tell them about being out there fishing?" Suzie asked.

"No, he was in a hurry and didn't know what had happened, but now that he knows, he's going to talk to Jason." Paul set his cup down on the dining room table and looked straight into Suzie's eyes.

"Are you sure he will?" Suzie met his eyes. "Don't you think we should tell Jason in case he doesn't?"

"No. I don't want to betray his trust. These guys trust me." Paul pointed at himself.

"So, you're willing to risk him not talking to Jason and letting Kendra's killer go free to keep your street credit?" Suzie raised her eyebrows.

"Street credit?" Paul laughed. "Let's not be dramatic about this."

"Ouch, that's not a good word to use." Mary turned and headed for the kitchen. "I think I'll let you two figure this out."

"Mary! Where are you running off to?" Wes' voice called out from the front door. "Don't disappear on me!" His jovial tone cut through the tension that had built up between Suzie and Paul.

"Wes." Paul offered him a relieved smile. "Here with an update?"

Mary spun around and smiled at the sight of Wes. She walked over to him.

"Morning. It's good to see you. Do you have any news?"

"Straight to the point." Wes chuckled as he pulled off his hat. "Yes. Unfortunately, it's not of an arrest. I did find out a little bit more about Kendra."

"Do tell." Suzie's eyes lingered on Paul a moment longer before she looked over at Wes. "Any news is good news at this point. So far it seems like a phantom must have killed her."

"I don't know about her killer being a phantom, but Kendra sure seemed to be one. The way she hid her past makes it very clear that she was on the run from something, or someone. Likely, the person who killed her." Wes lowered his voice. "These things never end well."

"These things?" Mary poured Wes a cup of coffee. "What do you mean?"

"I think it was someone who held a heavy grudge that committed the crime. Someone from her past, maybe. Maybe they hunted her down. I also think it's possible that she was on the run from the police." Wes took the coffee cup from Mary. "Thank you."

"So, you also don't think it could have been a random person that wanted to steal her bracelet?" Mary glanced over at Suzie. "I guess that might narrow things down."

"Oh, I still think it's possible, but less likely," Wes said.

"It could have been Will, if he was upset or furious about her taking the bracelet." Mary put a muffin on a plate and put it down in front of Wes.

"Yes." Suzie pursed her lips. "But if it was someone from her past, then where did they go? Did they really just swoop in long enough to kill her and then move along? If they planned this, why did they have to use the metal detector as a murder weapon?"

"That's true, where did they go? People don't exactly fly under the radar around here. If you're not a local, you'll get noticed real fast," Mary said.

"Maybe they are a local, and they knew her from the past." Wes had a sip of coffee.

"True." Suzie nodded. "But if it is someone new to town, there are only a few new people in town that I know about. Josh, and—"

"Lizzy?" Mary's eyes widened.

"Lizzy." Suzie looked over at Mary. "She was on the beach around the time of the murder, and we don't know much about her history."

"I've actually been digging more into Lizzy." Wes tapped his pen against the notepad. "Since she discovered the body and was one of the few people that we can confirm was on the beach around the time of Kendra's death, I've been combing through her information. I came across a red flag."

"You did?" Suzie leaned forward. "What?"

"The same red flag I found in Kendra's past. Lizzy has changed her name. It's hard to trace her history. It just seems too coincidental that they have that in common and ended up at the beach at around the same time. And one of them wound up dead." Wes finished off his muffin. "I haven't found an exact connection, yet, but I'm going to keep looking."

"So, maybe someone from Lizzy's past killed Kendra. They knew Lizzy was on the beach, from the ad. Maybe they killed Kendra to scare Lizzy. Or maybe they killed Kendra thinking it was Lizzy." Suzie leaned forward.

"It's possible. My hunch is that Lizzy and Kendra knew each other somehow from the past, and if I can find that they did and how they did, then we have a possible motive," Wes suggested.

"So, it could really be Lizzy." Suzie looked at Wes.

"It's definitely possible. I need to get this information to Jason. I just wanted to drop in here on the way to the station." Wes picked up another muffin. "For later?"

"Of course." Mary grabbed a couple of brown bags. "And take that to Jason." She popped a muffin in the bag.

"Thank you." Wes took the bags from her and put the muffin he had picked up in the empty one. "I'll update you as soon as I know anything." He turned toward the door.

"Paul, can you keep asking around the docks?

Maybe you'll turn up something." Suzie looked into his eyes.

"I'll see what I can find out." Paul walked toward the door.

CHAPTER 15

The moment Wes and Paul left, Suzie spun around to face Mary.

"I think we need to speak to Lizzy face-to-face before Jason gets to her. We can't tip her off that we know she's changed her name, because that may make her run before Jason has a chance to question her, but maybe we can find out something. She was so upset after the murder that she could barely get a few words out. What if all of that was an act? I'll be honest, I didn't even really consider the possibility that she could be involved."

"I didn't, either." Mary sighed. "She seemed so distraught."

"Not when we first got there. She didn't even scream. She wasn't even crying. Maybe she turned on the waterworks when we got there for our benefit."

"Maybe. What I thought was that she was just so shocked, and seeing us brought the reality of what had happened to the surface."

"She also wanted to leave. She didn't want to speak to the police." Suzie snapped her fingers.

"True. She moved here shortly after Kendra. But if she's someone from Kendra's past, wouldn't it be a very elaborate ruse to move here and pretend to start a yoga business?" Mary grabbed her purse and walked toward the door.

"Yes, I guess. Maybe she opened the business and then saw Kendra was here. It might have really been a coincidence. We know that she probably knew Kendra was here. She took a picture with Kendra in it. Remember?" Suzie grabbed her own purse and followed Mary. "We'll only find out more if we talk to her."

They put Pilot in the yard, then walked over to Mary's SUV.

"I know her address." Mary settled in the driver's seat, then looked over at Suzie. "I'm not sure what the best way is to approach this. If we come on too strong, she's not likely to share anything at all."

"But we have to say something to shake her up, right? Think about it, Mary. If all of those tears were an act, she's a master manipulator."

"True, we need to make sure we stay on our toes." Mary pulled out of the parking lot.

"She doesn't live too far from here, does she?"

"This is the street she lives on." Mary turned onto the street. "Yes, this should be her place right here." She parked in front of a small house. "And that's her car, so she's definitely home."

"Let's see what she has to say." Suzie stepped out of the car and led the way up to the door.

Mary looked over the small porch area of the house and noticed a pile of assorted shells, broken pieces of metal, and thin chains.

"Do you think those are from jewelry?" She nudged Suzie's arm as she pointed to the pile.

Before Suzie could answer her, the door swung open.

Lizzy stood in front of them, her cheeks stained with tears, and her eyes swollen and red.

"What is it?" She sniffled just before a sob shook her body. "Please, I can't see anyone right now."

"Lizzy, are you okay?" Mary noted how sad and tired she looked. Could she really be faking that? Was she so upset because she was the murderer?

"I can't calm down. I've tried everything. I listened to meditation music. I lit some candles and some incense. I did some stretching, and some exercise, but I can't stop thinking about what happened." Lizzy waved them away from the door. "Please, just go, I don't want anyone seeing me like this."

"Maybe you need people around you right now." Suzie took a step forward. "We just wanted to check on you. We know that you're new to town, and you might not know too many people, yet. After the shock that you've had, you shouldn't be alone."

"Exactly." Mary was a bit stunned by the empathy in Suzie's tone. Usually her take-no-prisoners attitude came across in a very different way. Much harsher. "Can we come inside for a little while? Maybe having some company will help you calm down."

"I don't think I'll ever be able to calm down." Lizzy stepped away from the door as she wiped her cheeks. "I moved here thinking I could start over, have a quiet life. I was so excited to start my business. I thought I would just lead a quiet, peaceful life here." She gulped down a deep breath. "And is it horrible of me to feel grateful that it was her and not me?" She clapped her hand over her mouth and shook her head. "I shouldn't have said that."

"It's okay, Lizzy." Mary stepped into the house and took Lizzy's hand. "We all have different feelings at a time like this." She looked into her eyes. "Just try to take a deep breath. Nice and slow. Real easy in, and then out just a little bit at a time."

"Thank you." Lizzy took another deep breath, following Mary's instructions. "That's really helping."

Suzie glanced over at Mary, then looked over the sparse furnishings in Lizzy's house.

"You really haven't been here long, have you? What brought you here, Lizzy?"

"What?" Lizzy sniffled.

"Of all of the towns that you could have moved to, was there a particular reason that you picked this one?" Suzie shrugged. "Just curious."

"It was pretty random. I'd seen some pictures posted online when a friend of mine visited the area, and the beach looked so beautiful, especially with Dune House as the backdrop. I just knew it was the place where I wanted to start over." Lizzy closed her eyes. "I guess I was very wrong about that. At this point, I might as well pack up my things and get ready to move on."

"Why would you say that?" Mary squeezed her hand. "You've made a home here."

"Have I? I can barely afford to buy things for my house, and after what happened on the beach just before what was supposed to be my first class, I don't think I'm going to get much interest in my yoga classes."

"You said something about wanting to feel safe here." Suzie wandered toward her. "Is that because you weren't safe before?"

"My hometown wasn't like this, that's for sure. It wasn't nearly as peaceful. Lots of crime. I made a few friends that just pretended to be friends. They were bad news, got involved in crime, and I didn't want to get caught up in that. I needed to get away." Lizzy clasped her hands together.

"That can be hard. I can understand why you would want a fresh start." Mary offered a sad smile. "And this has been a rough start. But I bet you can still turn it around."

"All I've been thinking about is what happened to Kendra. The police asked me so many questions that I couldn't answer." Lizzy frowned. "I just wish I could do something to help."

"Are you sure you didn't see anyone else on the

beach. Maybe a boat in the water?" Suzie searched her eyes.

"No, I didn't see anyone. Not Kendra. Not Jeanette, either. I went for a quick walk, then gathered all of my things from my car and went down to where I set up on the beach." Lizzy froze. "Actually, now that I think about it, I did hear something when I was near the parking lot when I first got there."

"You did?" Mary tightened her grip on Lizzy's hand. "What did you hear?"

"A click." Lizzy snapped the fingers of her free hand. "Like the sound of a picture being taken. It startled me. I was worried someone was taking a picture of me in my yoga gear. But when I looked around the parking lot, I didn't see anyone. I figured I'd just heard wrong. Could that be something?"

"Maybe. It's possible. We'll make sure that Jason knows about it," Suzie said.

"And you're sure you'd never met Kendra before?" Mary released her hand. "You did take her picture."

"Like I said, I took a picture of the beach, not of any particular person. I didn't know her." Lizzy's eyes flashed as she looked between them. "Why do you keep acting like I should know something? Do you suspect me?"

Suzie flinched as she felt the venom in Lizzy's gaze.

"No, I'm sorry if it feels that way. I think Mary and I are just eager to figure out what happened to Kendra, so we might be coming on a little strong. Sorry about that." She tipped her head toward the door. "We should be going."

"Yes, that's probably best." Lizzy followed them to the door. "I appreciate you stopping by, but really I think I'm better off trying to handle this myself. My emotions are so wild right now, and clearly I'm getting paranoid."

"If you need anything, please call us." Mary turned back to meet her eyes. "I just want you to know you're not alone here."

"Thanks." Lizzy forced a smile, then closed the door behind them.

CHAPTER 16

"Wow, Lizzy is very emotional." Suzie walked over to the car.

"She is. She picked up on us possibly suspecting her quickly. That could be a guilty conscience." Mary opened the driver's side door. "But the one thing she remembered, hearing a picture being taken, we might be able to do something with that."

"What?" Suzie settled in the passenger seat. "She said she didn't see anyone around."

"True. But maybe it will lead somewhere." Mary started the car.

"We should take a ride over to the police station and update Jason on all of this."

"All of it?" Mary pulled out onto the street. "Including the fisherman that Paul mentioned?"

"Maybe not all of it." Suzie clenched her jaw. "I know, it seems wrong to hold back information, but I don't want to betray Paul's trust. Hopefully, Pete will go to the police himself."

"But what if he doesn't. He might have seen something and not even realize it's important." Mary turned into the police station. "I know that you trust Paul. I trust him, too. But maybe he's being too trusting of this guy."

"Maybe. I will think about it, okay?"

"Okay." Mary parked in front of the police station. "I won't say a word about it. I'll leave that up to you."

"Thanks." Suzie held the door open for Mary.

After the officer at the front desk checked with Jason to make sure they could go through, Suzie followed Mary to the large room that Jason had set up for the investigation.

Jason looked up from his phone as they walked in.

"Any news is good news."

"I'm afraid it's not much." Suzie filled him in on their suspicions about Lizzy, and her recollection of a sound in the parking lot.

"This is good information. Thanks." Jason looked up at her.

"I presume Wes has spoken to you about Lizzy." Suzie pointed to the half-eaten muffin. "Are you going to bring her in?"

"No, not yet." Jason shook his head.

"If you know she's lying about her identity, isn't that enough to bring her in, now?" Suzie locked her eyes to his. "Why wait, Jason? She could be packing up to leave right now!"

"If I tip her off before I have any real evidence, then she'll have time to cover her tracks. At the moment, she doesn't think I really suspect her. I have a car watching her, and if she tries to take off, then they'll bring her in. The longer we leave her to her own devices, the better the chance that she will do something that will indicate her guilt." Jason leaned back against his chair.

"I see, yes, that's clever." Suzie gave a short nod. "But how long do you think it will take? If she really is the killer, I'd feel much better if she was behind bars sooner than later."

"It depends on how well she hid her past, and how well Kendra did. It's going to take some time to piece together their connection. If there even is a connection." Jason set his phone down on the table. "Right now, it's just a hunch. We have no proof they're connected."

"Wes mentioned that he thinks whoever killed Kendra must have had a personal relationship with her, and a lot of rage. He thinks it's probably someone from her past. Lizzy is also new in town. That's what led us to suspect her. But I'm not so sure she knew Kendra, after talking to her this afternoon." Mary leaned forward. "She didn't say much about her past, but she didn't exactly avoid talking about it, either."

"She didn't say where she was from, or exactly why she moved here. She told us a few little details, something about getting involved with the wrong crowd who became involved in crime, but nothing that would lead to any concrete information. Maybe it was because she was upset. Or maybe it was because she knew exactly how much to say, and how much not to say." Suzie held out one hand, then the other. "It's hard to know."

"Hopefully, I'll come across something more solid." Jason had a bite of muffin.

"I think Jeanette is still planning on leaving. I know that you'd rather she didn't. I just thought I should let you know." Suzie noticed Beth and Kirk approaching the conference room.

"Unfortunately, I can't do anything to keep her from leaving, at the moment. But it would definitely be better for the investigation if she stuck around. If you can do anything to encourage her to stay, I'd appreciate that."

"We'll try. Hopefully, we can get her to stay for at least one more night. I'll make a special dinner for her. But I'm not sure how much longer we can persuade her. She seemed pretty determined to get back home." Mary started toward the door.

"Thanks for the heads-up." Jason held open the door of the conference room for them. "Hopefully, we can get to the bottom of things soon. If you learn anything else, please keep me informed. But remember, this is a murder investigation, so watch your step."

"We will." Suzie followed Mary toward her car. "You know what, Mary? I think we should invite a few more people to that special dinner. Paul, Wes, and Lizzy. Maybe having everyone together will bring something to the surface."

"Good idea. You send the invites, and I'll plan the menu." Mary opened the door to the car and met Suzie's eyes across the top of it. "Do you really think we can get Jeanette to stay?"

"We'll have to try our best."

CHAPTER 17

Mary swayed slowly to the music that filled the kitchen. Cooking and baking had become one of her favorite escapes while she raised her children, no matter the chaos going on around her. Her kids were grown and lived in another state, and she rarely cooked for them anymore, but she still loved preparing food for people.

"Paul, Wes, Lizzy, and Jeanette all said they would be here to join us." Suzie leaned against the counter beside Mary and made sure to keep her voice down. "This could be a very interesting meal."

"It could be. I quickly did a check on the rooms to make sure that the guests have everything they need. No one is in at the moment." Mary sniffled as she sliced an onion. "Did you invite Josh?"

"Yes, I sent him a text. But he can't make it. He's working late."

"I don't know. It feels a little odd to be making a special dinner with all that's going on." Mary squeezed her eyes shut, then sniffled again.

"It's a good thing." Suzie patted her back as she brushed past her to collect a baking dish from one of the cabinets. "This roast will leave everyone feeling nourished. I'm sure Jeanette will appreciate it after all that she's been through since arriving here."

"And Lizzy could certainly benefit from being surrounded by new friends, since she's still new in town. She probably hasn't had the chance to make many." Mary began adding the onions to the baking dish that Suzie left on the counter for her. "All I can think is, who had the opportunity to kill Kendra? She wasn't dead for long, and the beach wasn't empty for long. Maybe someone was following her. Or maybe came to the beach with her. Don't you think?"

"Yes, maybe." Suzie's eyes locked to hers.

"But who would have come to the beach with her? All of her metal-detecting friends claim they weren't with her at the time of the murder." Mary raised her eyebrows as she continued to prepare the roast. "Of course, the killer isn't going to volunteer that they were with her at that time. I know Wes said that he thinks it might be someone from Kendra's past, but I'm not so sure. I think the best suspects are definitely Kendra's friends. Leanne had the job she wanted so desperately stolen right out from under her by Kendra, that's a pretty good motive."

"Leanne missing out on the job is a motive." Suzie set the oven to preheat, then began cleaning up the cutting board. "But is it enough? Would she really kill someone over a job loss? It's not like she can't get another one."

"It's not so easy these days to find a job, especially in a small town like this and in the off-season. And maybe it was more the betrayal of Kendra stealing the job, not the fact that she didn't get it." Mary added a few spices to the dish. "Plus, there might have been more conflict between them that she's not admitting to."

"That's true. We'll have to see if we can dig a little deeper into their relationship." Suzie glanced at the clock on the kitchen wall. "Paul should be here any minute."

"Wes texted me a few minutes ago that he's on

his way. I told him no shop talk tonight. I just want Jeanette and Lizzy to feel comforted, not interrogated. After the way Lizzy reacted this afternoon, I doubt that she'll stick around if she feels like she's being questioned. Plus, our main goal right now is to get Jeanette to stay." Mary slid the roast into the oven.

"It will be tough not to fire off some questions, but I'll try. It's hard not to want to grill them both for every detail." Suzie looked down at Pilot who had wandered into the kitchen the moment the meat had hit the heat in the oven. "Hey, buddy."

Pilot jumped up against her legs and gazed at her.

"I missed you, too." Suzie stroked the top of his head and rubbed his ears. "Leanne isn't the only one of Kendra's friends that had a motive, either." She lifted her eyes to Mary's. "That missing bracelet is a big motive."

"And even Leanne suspects Will of taking it. They're supposed to be friends. I think there's a lot to be suspicious about there," Mary said.

"Still, what Jason discovered about Lizzy's past does make me wonder if Wes might be onto something. What are the chances that two people end up on the same beach on the same day, who have a hidden past?" Suzie paused as Pilot ran toward the door.

A moment later, a swift knock, followed by Paul's voice, alerted them all to his presence.

"Something smells amazing." Paul stepped through the door with a wide grin. "Hi, boy." He stopped to pet Pilot, then continued forward to greet Suzie who had crossed the hallway to meet him.

"Oh dear, it's definitely not you." Suzie took a big step back as Paul reached for her.

"Oh no, right, sorry about that." Paul scrunched up his nose. "I should go get cleaned up. I was helping a friend out with his haul before I came over."

"A friend? As in the friend that was out on the water around the time of the murder?" Suzie followed him into the kitchen.

"No, not Pete. Shawn. But I just found out that Shawn was actually running on the beach that morning at around six. He's new to Garber and generally likes to keep to himself. I helped him with his haul and asked him if he'd seen anything or anyone." Paul glanced over at her as he began scrubbing his hands. "He said that he saw someone walking from the parking lot when he passed it, but he wasn't sure if it was Kendra or someone else. He didn't pay much attention to it. But said he didn't see Lizzy, Jeanette, Molly, or Michael. But he did see a guy out there, farther along the beach. He doesn't know his name, but he had curly, blond hair. He saw him on the docks, then on the beach. He said he looked quite young, maybe in his twenties." He gave his hands another thorough scrub.

"That sounds like it could be our guest Josh. But he claims he was sleeping the whole time." Suzie frowned. "Has Shawn spoken to the police about this?"

"He didn't want to deal with the police. I think he has a criminal past. He spoke to me on condition I won't give the police his name. Otherwise, he probably wouldn't have said a word about it." Paul dried his hands.

"He didn't want to deal with the police?" Mary repeated his words in an incredulous tone. "What is it about your friends and the police? This is a murder. He needs to talk to them. Is he some kind of criminal?"

"I don't know about his past." Paul's tone hardened a degree, then he cleared his throat. "Listen, we can tell Jason about someone looking like Josh possibly being on the beach and leave

Shawn's name out of it. It doesn't make a difference if we don't tell Jason who told us."

"Actually, it does. He needs to tell Jason he was on the beach. It means that there was another potential killer on the beach," Suzie said.

"Look, I mentioned that it would be a good idea for him to speak to Jason, and he almost threw me off his boat. So, be glad I'm still around for dinner." Paul winked at her.

"I don't like this guy one bit, and if I see him, he'll be the one going flying over the side of the boat." Suzie crossed her arms.

"Relax, relax." Paul smiled as he held his hands out to her. "Do I pass the smell test, yet?"

"I would love you no matter what you smelled like." Suzie laughed. "But yes, this is much better."

"Good." Paul smiled.

"Is there any chance that Shawn is lying? Maybe he knows Josh is staying with us, and he's trying to divert suspicion away from himself. He could be the person we're looking for. He did threaten to hurt you, after all." Suzie shrugged.

"No, he was just joking. I don't think he would hurt me. I don't think he did this. He doesn't seem like someone who would do this. I haven't known him long, but I think I know him well enough to know that he's not a killer," Paul said.

"You know him well enough to know that he probably has a past he wants to keep hidden." Suzie held his gaze. "I don't think that makes him innocent."

"Hi, everyone!" Wes called out from the front door as Pilot ran toward him.

CHAPTER 18

"Wes, come on in. The roast still has some time to go, but I've put some snacks out." Mary smiled at him as he ruffled Pilot's fur.

"You're too good to me, Mary. Always keeping me fed." Wes patted his stomach. "Not so good for the waistline, I'm afraid."

"You look great. Oh, I should turn off the music!" Mary hurried toward the kitchen.

"Not yet, you shouldn't." Wes caught her around the waist and spun her back to face him. "May I have this dance?"

"Wes, I don't know." Mary started to pull away.

"Please?" Wes gazed into her eyes with a soft smile.

"All right, but just one quick dance." Mary laughed.

Wes guided her through a few sways and spins.

Suzie glanced over at Paul.

"Are you going to ask me to dance?" Paul smiled as he winked at her.

"No, I'm going to ask you to tell me where to find Shawn's boat, so I can go see him." Suzie locked her eyes to his.

"I really don't want you to speak to him, Suzie. I don't know him that well. What if I've got it wrong and he really is a murderer?"

"I can take care of myself." Suzie crossed her arms.

"I know you can." Paul looked into her eyes. "But let me speak to him again first. Let me see if he'll go talk to Jason, okay?"

"Okay. But if he doesn't, I want to speak to him. Agreed?" Suzie wrapped her arms around him.

"Agreed." Paul kissed her cheek.

"What's going on in here?" Jeanette stood at the entrance to the kitchen. She looked from Wes and Mary dancing to Suzie and Paul hugging. "Am I going to be a fifth wheel? Is this some kind of romantic dinner?"

"No, it's not. I'm sorry, Jeanette." Mary pulled away from Wes. "We just got a little caught up in the moment. Dinner is almost ready. There are some crackers and cheese and things on the table if you're hungry now."

"Sure, thanks." Jeanette looked between them again. "What about wine? Is there any of that?"

"Plenty." Suzie held up two bottles. "White or red?"

"White, please." Jeanette pointed at the bottle.

"I'll pour you a glass." Mary grabbed a glass.

Soon, the five were assembled around the dinner table, each with a drink in their hands. Just as the oven timer rang, the front door swung open, and Lizzy stepped inside.

"Am I late?" Lizzy hovered near the door.

"Not at all, Lizzy, come on in. Take a seat. I'll get you a glass of wine." Mary stood up from the table. "I'm just bringing dinner out now."

"No wine for me. I'll just have water, thanks." Lizzy sat down at the table.

"I'll pour you some." Paul picked up the water bottle in the middle of the table.

"I'll help you, Mary." Wes stood up and followed her into the kitchen.

Lizzy stared hard at her empty plate.

"I'm so glad you were able to join us, Lizzy." Suzie smiled at her. "I know it's been a rough couple of days."

"That's an understatement." Lizzy continued to stare at her plate.

"Can't get it out of your head, huh?" Jeanette took a big swallow of her glass of wine. "I know the feeling."

Mary set the roast down on the table.

Lizzy burst into tears.

"I should have helped her! I should have gotten there earlier!"

"Oh, Lizzy." Mary rubbed her hand along Lizzy's shoulders. "Even if you were there, think about it, what could you have done?" Her voice softened. "Whoever did this to Kendra was obviously very strong."

"Maybe, but I know how to defend myself." Lizzy shrugged. "I'm well-trained in martial arts. Yoga is my new passion, but I still have the skills and know how to protect myself. I'm sure that if I had been there, I would have been able to protect Kendra."

"Really?" Suzie leaned a little closer to her.

"What prompted you to go from martial arts to yoga."

"Let's just say, life changes." Lizzy's voice hardened.

Suzie and Mary exchanged a brief glance.

"Well, I for one wish I had never left my bed. If I had just stayed in bed I would have missed the whole thing. Instead, I ended up in the middle of it. I still have the police hounding me." Jeanette held up her phone. "I've told them everything I know. And now they're saying I shouldn't leave town? What's that about?"

"The detective really needs anyone who might have been a witness to stick around at least for another day or two to make sure that he has all of the evidence he needs." Suzie reached for the serving fork and gathered a few slices of roast and vegetables onto her plate. "I understand that it's pretty inconvenient for you."

"It's not really the inconvenience that's the problem. It's the fact that I didn't see anything, and they keep acting like I did." Jeannette piled some food onto her plate as well. "I keep thinking about every second I spent out on the beach. Did I hear something? See something? Did I somehow block it out?" She sighed. "But there's nothing. I just went for a run, like I always do. I just took my time and enjoyed the beach. I had no idea that someone was being killed a short distance away. How could I?"

"I know it's hard. But you did remember hearing someone, right? That was something new," Mary said.

"Yes, it was. But it doesn't mean anything." Jeanette shrugged.

"You heard someone?" Lizzy looked across the table at her. "Who?"

"I think it was Kendra." Jeanette poked at her food but didn't take a bite.

"Really? But I didn't hear anyone!" Lizzy's voice raised. "I was right there! How could you hear someone when I didn't?"

"I don't know. Maybe it was before you came to the beach. I didn't see you there. It would have been shortly after seven. I'm not even sure what I heard. My music stopped between songs, and I thought I heard something." Jeannette closed her eyes. "We don't even know when she was murdered exactly. Maybe I'm just so desperate to join the dots that I imagined it."

"I'm sure that's not the case. It just might have been something else, not Kendra." Mary studied Jeanette's full plate. "But you should try to eat something, Jeanette. If you don't like the roast, I can make you something else if you'd like? We have a full pantry and fridge. Just name it, and I'm sure I can whip it up."

"No!" Jeanette's sharp tone drew a harsh look from Wes. "I'm sorry." Her voice faltered as his gaze remained on her. "It's just that I don't feel like eating. It was so kind of you to make this dinner, and I thought I would be able to enjoy it, but it all just feels so strange. I don't want to sit around talking about a murder. I don't want to be part of any of this." She stood up from the table. "I'm just going to go for a walk. I need to clear my head."

"You're going to go out there alone?" Lizzy looked up at her. "Aren't you scared? Whoever killed Kendra could still be out there."

"No, I'm not scared." Jeanette looked at her. "It's pretty clear that this wasn't random. Kendra did something to get herself into that situation. It's not like she was this saint that no one would want to hurt. Someone wanted her dead."

"Well, we don't know that for sure." Paul watched her as she moved toward the sliding glass doors.

"It might be better if you didn't go out alone,

Jeanette." Wes' concerned tone drew the attention of everyone still at the table. "You're upset."

"I'll be fine." Jeanette opened the door. "I don't need anyone telling me what to do."

"All right, how about some company instead?" Lizzy stood up from the table. "I can't eat, either. Maybe we could walk together?"

Jeanette looked over her shoulder at Lizzy for a long moment. The hardness in her eyes faded as she gave a slow nod.

"I guess I wouldn't mind some company."

"Maybe we should all go?" Suzie stood up.

"No, please stay. Enjoy your meal." Jeanette looked over the gathering of people at the table. "I know I've ruined this wonderful dinner you prepared. I'm just not up for it. You four should enjoy it." She held the door open for Lizzy. "We'll be fine."

Lizzy hesitated for a moment, then took a deep breath, and stepped through the door.

Suzie and Mary watched them go. The moment the door clicked shut, Suzie looked around the table.

"I don't know if that's such a good idea."

"Maybe not, but they're free to make their own

choices. There's no stopping them." Paul picked up his fork.

As they shared the remainder of the meal, Suzie felt a jolt of anxiety. The thought of the two women on the beach made her wonder about Kendra's last moments. Had she really been with someone she trusted? Why hadn't she tried to protect herself?

CHAPTER 19

When Suzie awoke the next morning, for an instant she couldn't recall if Jeanette and Lizzy had returned from their walk. Her pounding heart slowed as she remembered them returning unharmed the night before.

Josh had come home shortly after them. Before she could ask him any questions about the morning of the murder, he said he didn't want any food and headed to bed.

Suzie descended the stairs and walked into the kitchen to find Mary leaning against the counter beside the coffee maker.

Pilot ran over to Suzie with his tail wagging.

"You're full of beans." Suzie knelt down and let Pilot kiss her cheek. "It's good to see you."

"How did you sleep?" Mary lifted her tired gaze to Suzie's.

"Restlessly. My mind couldn't stop trying to sort through what we know about the murder." Suzie grabbed a coffee cup and stepped up beside Mary.

"I know. I barely slept at all." Mary had a sip of coffee. "I just want this murder solved so we can move on."

"Okay, let's get it solved. What's next, then? We don't have any new clues, do we?"

"Maybe not new. But we do have one clue we can follow as a start." Mary grabbed the coffee and filled Suzie's cup, then her own. "We know that Kendra's bracelet went missing. And we know who likely took it."

"Will?" Suzie murmured a thank-you for the coffee, then blew across the hot liquid.

"Yes. Wes had us focused on Kendra's past, but her present might be where we can find some good information. We know that she always wore the diamond bracelet. We know that it wasn't found with her body. We know that her skin was irritated as if she'd been wearing a bracelet. All of that points to one person." Mary sipped her coffee.

"Will." Suzie nodded. "If that's the case, then I say we should pay him another visit."

"My thoughts exactly." Mary picked up her purse. "I've just been waiting for you to get up."

"Really?" Suzie laughed as she collected her own purse. "I would have been happy for you to wake me."

"I thought about it, but I took Pilot for a walk instead." Mary led the way to the front door.

"Wait, what?" Suzie caught up with her as she crossed the threshold. "You went out onto the beach alone?"

"Not alone, with Pilot." Mary crossed the porch and descended the stairs.

"Mary!" Suzie matched her pace. "What were you thinking? How could you go out on your own like that?"

"I was thinking that Jeanette was right." Mary pulled open the driver's side door of her SUV. "I don't think Kendra ended up dead because someone came across her and decided to kill her. We know two things about her. We know that she snaked a job out from under someone who was supposed to be a friend. We know that she broke the rules of the club she belonged to and refused to share her good fortune. Not only that, but she flaunted it." She slid into the driver's seat.

"So, you're saying Kendra wasn't the greatest

person in the world?" Suzie settled into the passenger seat.

"I'm not one to judge. People have their reasons for doing things. What I'm saying is that she was no stranger to making people angry. And from the way she was killed, we believe that whoever killed her most likely knew her and was quite determined to do so and motivated by some fierce anger. Jason believes this was personal. A targeted attack." Mary started the car and pulled out of the parking lot. "So yes, I felt safe walking on the beach. Plus, I had Pilot."

"He's a great protector, isn't he?" Suzie smiled.

"Absolutely. It looks like someone is waiting for us." Mary put the car in park and pulled out the key as Will stepped out of a small garden shed. His eyes widened, then he quickly walked back inside. A few seconds later, he walked out again and headed toward his house.

"That was weird," Suzie mumbled.

They stepped out of the car and walked toward him.

Will greeted the two of them with a scowl.

"What are you doing here?" He turned away from them and started up the porch stairs.

"Just stopping by." Suzie approached him with a confident stride.

"Not up for visitors." Will stepped into the house and started to close the door.

"Just a second, please?" Suzie put her foot against the door before he could close it. "We're not here to bother you, just to talk."

"Listen, I'm just trying to live my life in peace. Is that such a terrible thing?" Will brushed a stray strand of silver hair back behind his ear. "I'm retired, and I just want to mind my own business and putter around. I didn't expect to be swept up in any kind of murder investigation. I'm sorry that Kendra is dead, really I am, but it has nothing to do with me." He began to try to force the door shut.

"I understand that you don't want to be bothered." Suzie settled her gaze on his. "It just surprises me, that's all."

"Surprises you?" Will paused just inside the door and stared back out at her. "What surprises you?"

"Oh, just that you don't seem to want her murder solved." Suzie shrugged.

"I do want it solved. But I have a lot to deal with." Will swept his gaze over the assortment of broken tools and furniture piled on the side of his porch.

"You do have a beautiful home here." Suzie glanced over at Mary, then looked back at him.

"It is. It's a bit small. I know it looks a bit messy and like I'm struggling, but I do my best." Will continued to focus on Suzie. "As you know, I'm retired. I don't have a lot of money to live on."

"We can see that you're doing the best you can with what you have." Mary smiled.

"I am." Will's voice took on a note of pride.

"It must have really upset you when Kendra wouldn't share the money from the bracelet with you." Suzie locked her eyes to his. "It would go a long way in helping you financially. Are you sure you didn't take it? We would understand if you did."

"Oh, you're a tricky one, aren't you!" Will glared at her. "That's what this has been about this whole time? That stupid bracelet!" He slapped his hand against the doorjamb. "I told the police, I don't know anything about it."

"But Kendra had it on her all the time, right?" Suzie raised her eyebrows.

"Sure, I guess." Will coughed. "Like I said, it has nothing to do with me."

"But it does. I would think that knowing she died with something that valuable in her possession, you'd be pretty determined to get it back, especially since you believe she cheated you out of it in the first place." Suzie shrugged. "But have you even asked the police for it, or even gone looking for it?"

"You get on out of here." Will waved his hand at her. "You're just trying to stir up trouble. I want nothing to do with any of it." He jerked the door shut.

Suzie took a step back as the slam of the door caught her off guard.

"You definitely got under his skin, Suzie."

"Maybe, but not enough to get him to admit to anything." Suzie started to turn back toward the car.

"Suzie, wait." Mary caught her arm before she could take another step. "We should look over there." She pointed to the shed. The door hung open, barely attached by a rusted hinge. "He walked back in there after he saw us. Maybe to hide something that he didn't want us to see?"

"Maybe something like a diamond gold bracelet." Suzie glanced back at the front door of the house, then she looked over at Mary. "I can tell you that Jason will need a search warrant, and he doesn't have enough to get one. But there's nothing stopping a couple of nosy neighbors from taking a look. Right?"

CHAPTER 20

"Be my lookout!" Mary headed straight toward the door.

"Mary, wait, maybe you should be my lookout." Suzie followed her.

"Stay back!" Mary waved her off. "I can handle this." She nudged the door of the garden shed all the way open with the toe of her shoe. She stood in the doorway as she pulled out her phone and turned on the flashlight. As she aimed it at the contents of the shed, she took a sharp breath. "I definitely see something shiny in here."

"Is it the bracelet?" Suzie kept her eyes on the front door of the house.

"It's either the bracelet, or a really fancy piece of costume jewelry. I'm going to take a picture." Mary stayed in the doorway. She aimed her phone at the bracelet and took several snapshots. "Do you think I should grab it?"

"No, don't. If you take it, we won't be able to prove that Will had it this whole time. We can send the picture to Jason. He'll know what to do. Mary, Will's coming back outside." Suzie stepped forward as Will looked in their direction.

"Hey! What are you two doing? That's my property! You can't be near there!" Will rushed toward them.

"Just relax, Will." Suzie stepped in front of Mary before he could reach her. "We know you have the bracelet. You'd better think hard about what you do next before you end up in jail for murder."

"Oh, you found the bracelet, huh?" Will scowled at them both. "Well, I saw you put it in there. I guess you two are the ones who will end up standing trial for trying to frame me."

"Jason is on his way." Mary slipped her phone into her back pocket. "Will, you need to think this through. We didn't touch that bracelet. But Jason will check it for fingerprints. Whose do you think he will find?"

"We know you stole it, Will!" Suzie glared at

him. "Did you really murder her over it? Did you pull it off her after you killed her?"

"No," Will shrieked the word, then slammed his hands against the side of the garden shed. "No, I didn't kill her. They aren't going to lock me up for that!"

Jason's car screeched to a halt in the driveway. He jumped out with his hand on the butt of his gun.

"Will, put your hands in the air and back away!" Jason's commanding tone left no room for argument.

Will held up his hands but remained where he stood.

"You can't do this!" Will shouted. "You can't arrest me for something I didn't do!"

"The bracelet is in your shed, Will. Are you really going to still try to deny stealing it?" Suzie stared at him.

Jason walked over and looked through the open door of the shed.

"No, I'm not." Will's shoulders slumped. "Yes, I took the bracelet. Okay? I don't consider it stealing, though, because it belonged to me, too. I took it because I knew she was going to have it appraised, and it would be the one time that she wouldn't have it on because she cleaned it to get it appraised. I thought if I had it and then offered to split the profits with her, she would see reason. But I didn't expect her to die."

"You didn't expect her to die? So, it was okay to steal from her?" Jason asked.

"Like I said, I didn't consider it stealing when I took the bracelet." Will crossed his arms. "I didn't expect any of this to happen."

"So, you decided to lie to the police? To me?" Jason glared at him. "This whole time you had a piece of evidence that could make a difference in a murder investigation, and you withheld and lied about that evidence?"

"I didn't kill her. Okay?" Will's voice trembled. "But I knew if I told you that I had the bracelet, you wouldn't believe that. You would just think I killed her. But I didn't. I didn't!"

Suzie noticed someone on the sidewalk in front of Will's house. She quickly realized it was Larry.

"What's going on?" Larry looked at Will. "What did you do, Will? Did you kill her?"

"No, of course not." Will narrowed his eyes. "I just took the bracelet. You know it belonged to me as well?"

"I can't believe you did that. How could you?" Larry's voice wavered.

"I didn't do anything wrong," Will snapped as Larry stomped off down the street.

"You're going to have to come down to the station with me to discuss this." Jason took a step closer to Will. "Can we be civil about this?"

"What does it matter?" Will flung his hands into the air. "You're never going to believe me."

"Let's figure all of that out at the station." Jason led him to his car. He opened the back door and helped Will inside. Then he closed the door behind him.

"Aren't you going to arrest him?" Suzie watched Jason retrieve an evidence bag from the trunk of his car.

"I'd rather discuss things with him first. I think I'll get more out of him that way." Jason used the bag to pick up the bracelet, then sealed it closed. He looked between the two of them. "I don't think I have to tell you about the risk you took here, not just to your own lives, but to the integrity of my investigation."

"We couldn't just leave it there for him to hide, Jason. We saw it from the doorway." Suzie crossed her arms. "We did the only thing we could think to do. We made sure that you would be able to get your hands on it."

"Yes, you did. But a good lawyer could rip this apart. Still, this has definitely changed things." Jason turned back toward the car.

Suzie looked through the window as Will rocked forward and pressed his head against the seat in front of him.

"Do you think he did it, Jason?"

"It doesn't matter what I think, only what the evidence shows." Jason met her eyes for a moment. "But I think I might be a lot closer to finding out who is responsible for Kendra's death." He nodded to them both, then walked over to his car.

Suzie and Mary watched as Jason backed down the driveway.

"We knew he had the bracelet, didn't we? So why do I feel so surprised that we found it?" Mary asked.

"Something just doesn't feel right, does it?" Suzie walked over to Mary's car. "And without a confession, or a way to prove that Kendra was wearing the bracelet on Saturday morning, it's still not going to lead to an arrest for Kendra's murder."

"We're getting somewhere, but we're not there, yet."

"Let's go check in with Leanne. I'm curious to see how she'll react to the bracelet being found."

"Maybe she'll be at the library." Mary opened the driver's side door.

"I'll send Louis a text to check." Suzie sat down in the passenger seat. She nodded as Louis replied straight away. "Yes, she's there."

"All right, I'm going to make one quick stop first. If we want her to start talking, I think I know the best way to get that to happen."

CHAPTER 21

After a quick stop at the local nursery, Suzie and Mary walked into the library.

Leanne looked up from the computer at the front desk and watched as they walked toward her.

"It looks like you're settling in well." Mary smiled as she set a plant down on the desk. "Something to congratulate you on the new position."

"Oh wow, that's very kind of you." Leanne gazed at the plant with a faint smile. "It's hard to celebrate, even though I really wanted and needed this job. Obviously, getting it this way makes it hard to be happy about it."

"I can imagine," Suzie said.

"I heard you were at Will's house. Larry just

called to tell me he was walking past and he saw the police, and Will had the bracelet." Leanne's voice shook.

"So, your suspicions were right." Suzie nodded. "About Will, and the bracelet. We found it in his garden shed. Not hidden very well, actually."

"He told me that he didn't take it!" Leanne sank back in her chair. "And I believed him. I really did. I can't believe I believed him." Her cheeks reddened as she looked back at Suzie. "Are you saying that he killed Kendra?"

"No, we're not saying that." Mary settled her gaze on Leanne. "As of now, all we know is that he took the bracelet. He said he took it when she wasn't wearing it because she was going to get it appraised. Which would mean that she wasn't wearing it the morning she was murdered. Which pretty much eliminates robbery as the motive for her murder. But if he lied once about not taking the bracelet, I would guess that he could be lying about the fact that she wasn't wearing it when he took it. You know him better than either of us, though. What do you think?"

"I don't know. I just don't know." Leanne stared at the plant again. "She wasn't wearing it that morning, then? You're sure?"

"We're not sure. Mary just said that. We can only go with what Will said, but of course he's not very reliable since he's lied a few times already. That's why we're asking you. Do you think he's capable of killing Kendra to get his hands on that bracelet?" Suzie tapped her hand against the desk as Leanne's eyes glazed over. "Leanne, please, this is very important. I know you don't want to think the worst about your friend, but Kendra was your friend, too, wasn't she? Don't you want her murderer found?"

"Yes, she was my friend." Leanne's eyes misted with tears. "They both were. I just don't know how this could have happened. We all had so much fun together. Until she found that bracelet. That's when everything changed. It even made us hold off on recruiting new members, because of the tension between the group. I asked her once why she wore it all the time. I told her I could tell that it bothered Will. I asked her why she didn't care that it upset him."

"And? Did she explain it to you?" Mary asked.

"She told me it was the only way she felt she could keep it safe. She was constantly worried that someone, especially Will, would steal it. She said that she planned to wear it until the day she sold it, so that if it went missing, everyone would know—" Leanne's voice broke. She fell silent.

"Everyone would know what?" Mary's gentle voice filled the sudden quiet.

"Everyone would know that someone had pried it out of her cold dead hands," Leanne whispered her words as she shivered. "But it was just a joke. It's just something that people say. She didn't really mean that."

"Maybe not, but maybe she did mean it when she said she only felt safe wearing it. Which makes me wonder if Will really had the opportunity to steal it because she wasn't wearing it." Suzie took a step back. "The police are speaking to him now. Maybe they'll get to the bottom of this."

"I can't believe the police have taken him in." Leanne's voice wavered. "Poor Will, he must be terrified."

"It looks like Kendra was probably with someone she trusted that morning. Someone she never would have expected to do her harm." Suzie leaned forward. "It sounds to me like she might have been with a friend. I'm not sure she would have been that trusting around Will since you just said that she was worried he would try to steal the bracelet. Who would she have trusted?"

HOBBIES AND HOMICIDE

"Oh, are you talking about me? You think I'm a suspect?" Leanne pointed at herself. "Yes, I think she trusted me. We didn't know each other very long, of course, but she was my friend. But I didn't do this. I never would have hurt her. You can't really suspect me. I can't imagine who could have done this to her."

"And you don't think it was Will?" Suzie asked.

"I mean, I don't know. I can't imagine him doing something like this. I know that Will must be very upset. If he killed Kendra, I hope he gets locked up, but if he didn't, I just feel so sorry for him. He must feel terrible about all of this." Leanne stood up from her chair. "Please, I really need this job, and this is very upsetting."

"We understand." Mary caught Suzie's arm. "We'll be on our way."

"I had more questions for her, Mary," Suzie said as Mary led her out of the library.

"I know." Mary turned to face her. "But I didn't want to upset her more. She might be a suspect, but she just lost her friend."

"Her friend, exactly. Kendra wouldn't have trusted Will, but she would have trusted Leanne. Think about it, Mary. Will insists that he didn't kill

Kendra. Maybe he didn't. Maybe he wasn't the friend that was with Kendra that morning."

"But why would Leanne do it? Over the job? I don't know, I just don't think that's enough motive."

"Over the job. Over Kendra wearing the bracelet around Will. Over their club being ruined because Kendra wouldn't share." Suzie held up her fingers as she listed the reasons. "It's not always easy to come up with what we believe is a good motive, but we don't know how deeply someone feels about things. We can't eliminate Leanne. She was one of the closest people to Kendra."

"As close as Kendra would let someone be, in her new life." Mary glanced back over her shoulder at the library. "I'm just not sure if I can picture Leanne doing this."

"Well, unless Will confesses, I think she might just be our best suspect. Maybe Kendra discovered that Will had stolen her bracelet, and threatened to go to the police. You heard the way that Leanne reacted to Will being in custody. Maybe there's more going on between the two of them than we realized. People always have secrets, Mary." Suzie settled into the passenger seat of the car. "Let's go back to the house. I definitely need a second cup of coffee."

162

CHAPTER 22

As Mary turned into the parking lot of Dune House, she smiled at the sight of a familiar car.

"It looks like Wes is waiting for us." She parked and stepped out of the car.

Wes waved to them from the large front porch.

"I didn't expect you two to be out so early this morning, but I guess I should have known better." Wes smiled as he kissed Mary's cheek.

"We had some investigating to do." Suzie patted his shoulder as she stepped past him. "We solved one part of the case at least."

"So I've heard." Wes followed them inside. "Jason took Will in after you found the missing bracelet in his shed, right?"

"Right, but he still claims he had nothing to do with her murder." Suzie tossed down her purse, then crouched down to greet Pilot. "He must know that the police don't have enough evidence to arrest him. At least not yet, otherwise they would have already. They wouldn't have just taken him in for questioning."

"They don't even have enough to arrest him for theft." Wes took Mary's purse from her and hung it on a hook near the front door. "Technically, there's no way to prove that he stole the bracelet from Kendra. He could easily claim that she gave it to him. He could also claim that he owned it since he had been with her when she found it, which would mean it wasn't really theft. But, of course, that wouldn't be a very good argument."

"Okay, okay." Mary wiped her hands along her cheeks. "The reality is the bracelet doesn't matter. That's not what we want the truth about. Yes, he might have taken it. But did he kill her for it? That's the real question."

"I wonder, if he threatened her, wouldn't she have just given it to him?" Suzie sat down at the table and closed her eyes. "Yes, he was probably very aggravated by the fact that she broke the rules and wouldn't share the find with him. He also had to see her wearing it all the time. That had to really rub him the wrong way. But it was just a bracelet. The question is, was there something going on in his life to make it worth killing her to get it?"

"I did get a chance to go through his financial history, at least what's available to the public and to view without a warrant. His credit score is quite low. There's a lien on his house. I also found out that he had an operation a few months ago, so there might be some serious medical bills associated with that. I'd say his financial status is pretty dire, and that's only what I was able to discover on the surface. There might be more to find if Jason gets a warrant to dig deeper." Wes pulled a chair out from the table for Mary to sit on.

"Okay, so his life is going down the drain, and suddenly he discovers actual, genuine treasure. But because Kendra feels they didn't find it together, he loses out on it. That bracelet could have potentially changed his life for the better. That's a pretty strong motive." Suzie leaned back in her chair and stretched her legs out in front of her. "But does it make him the murderer? It would have taken a lot of rage to deliver those blows."

"Don't forget, Leanne said that she didn't believe that Kendra really even needed the job at the library. She said she never seemed to have any financial trouble. And before she applied for the job, as far as we know, she wasn't employed in this area, right?" Mary settled into the chair and patted Wes' hand as he settled it on her shoulder. "So, where is her money coming from? And if Will knew that she had no money troubles, then it probably made him even angrier that she refused to share the find. That could drive some pretty strong rage."

"True." Suzie tapped her fingertips against the table. "So, you have Will who is facing a dire financial situation, and he's watching Kendra live the good life with no job, no other visible means of income, and refusing to share her good fortune with him. Yes, I could see that building into fury. But a part of him had to know that if he killed her and took the bracelet, people would find out, right? He'd be the first person that they would suspect. Leanne suspected him of taking it, right away."

"It's possible that he wasn't thinking clearly." Wes sat down in the chair beside Mary's. "We've profiled the murder as being an impulsive kill. The murderer didn't come there with the murder weapon. They took it from her instead, and used it to kill her. But from the nature of the murder, there's also an indication that the murderer might have been driven by rage, maybe by a past grudge."

"From what I understand, they believe Kendra likely knew and trusted the person who killed her. That would explain why she didn't fight back. She didn't expect them to kill her." Suzie's voice trailed off. "I can't imagine the shock that she must have felt if it really was Will who killed her."

"But would she really be that shocked? Leanne mentioned earlier that Kendra was worried Will would try to steal the bracelet, so she wouldn't have trusted him." Mary patted Pilot's head.

"No, but she wouldn't have expected him to kill her. Right? There's a big difference between thinking someone might want to take something from you, and thinking that someone might want to take your life." Suzie stood up, walked into the kitchen, then poured a cup of coffee. "Wes, Mary, would you like any?"

"No, thanks. I want to go and do more research. I just wanted to stop by and check in with you. I'm hitting a lot of dead ends digging into Kendra's past. I'm going to look again. Something has to turn up eventually, right?" Wes looked between them.

"If anyone can find it, I'm sure it's you." Mary kissed him. "Thanks for checking in, Wes."

"I'll let you know if I find anything else." Wes waved to them as he headed to the door.

"Maybe we're missing something, too. We've been looking through Kendra's recent past, trying to make connections, but it's pretty clear that she didn't want people to get to know her very well. Leanne, on the other hand, has a lot of local connections, and she seems to be more willing to discuss her life. Maybe she posted things about her and Kendra." Suzie pulled out her phone. "Let's see if there's anything interesting."

"Good idea." Mary scooted her chair closer to the chair that Suzie sat down in. Together they looked through the posts that Leanne had made. "Oh look, she posted about a big find. That must be the bracelet." She pointed to the picture of Leanne and Kendra together. "They do look very friendly there, don't they?"

"Yes. Everything that Leanne posted indicates that they were good friends. As rocky as our conversation with Leanne was this morning, I think we need to talk to her again. She may be our only link to whatever Kendra was hiding."

"She claims that Kendra didn't tell her anything about her past." Mary looked up at her. "Do you think she's lying?"

"Maybe. Or maybe she may not realize that she has information that might help. It's worth a try. We have no other direction to go in at the moment. The only problem is, will she be willing to talk to us again?"

"I think I can make that happen." Mary smiled as she pulled out her own phone.

CHAPTER 23

After a quick check of Leanne's social media, Mary invited her to the local café for tea. From her profile, it looked like she often went there. Mary ordered Leanne's favorite tea before she even arrived.

"I hope this works." Suzie glanced around the crowded café.

"It looks like it did." Mary waved to Leanne as she stepped through the door.

"Thanks so much for meeting us here." Suzie paused as a waitress walked toward their table with a tray containing three cups of tea.

"Oh, I love the tea here." Leanne narrowed her eyes. "I'm not sure how you knew that." She sat down at the table with them.

"Happy coincidence?" Mary smiled as the waitress set the cups down on the table. "I wasn't sure if you'd want to talk to us more, after this morning. I know it might feel like we're asking too much of you." She slid the cup of tea closer to Leanne as she offered a small smile. "But we've asked a lot of people a lot of questions, and it's become clear that you were really Kendra's closest friend around here. So, you're probably our best source of information."

"Source of information?" Leanne picked up her cup. "Does that mean you're not considering me a suspect anymore?"

"I don't think we ever really did. Did we, Mary?" Suzie glanced over at her, then looked back at Leanne. "But we have known from the beginning that we could rely on you to help us solve your friend's murder. Even after she betrayed you by snatching that job out from under your nose."

"It wasn't a betrayal." Leanne pursed her lips. "Not exactly anyway. There aren't exactly a lot of job opportunities around here. I can understand that she decided to jump on the chance."

"But why?" Suzie raised her eyebrows. "Why would she want a job at the library and risk upsetting you to get it when, like you said before, she didn't seem to need the money?"

"I guess just for something to do, to keep her busy." Leanne had a sip of tea.

"But didn't you ever wonder why she didn't need to work? Not too many people her age are able to just live life without some kind of job to sustain them." Mary scooted her chair closer. "Did you ever ask her where she got all of her money from?"

"We did discuss it, sure." Leanne cleared her throat. "The first time I mentioned it she told me that she had inherited a fairly large sum of money from a family member. An aunt. She said she barely knew her, but she ended up leaving her money to her."

"I know a little something about that." Suzie smiled. "I inherited Dune House from my estranged uncle."

"I know." Leanne met Suzie's eyes. "I was satisfied with that answer, but another time she said that she had won a lawsuit. I figured maybe neither of those answers were the truth, and she just didn't really want to tell me."

"Two different stories. Interesting." Suzie tapped the side of her cup of tea. "Did she ever give any other explanation?"

"Once, when we went out for drinks, she had a few more than she planned to. I offered to drive her home. On the way, she talked about how much she liked being friends with me, and how important it is to be able to trust someone." Leanne picked up her cup and took a sip. "Then she said she had betrayed some people's trust once, and that's how she had so much money. She promised she would never do that to me. But I guess that was a lie, too, because she did end up applying for the job I wanted. The job I needed."

"People are usually more honest when they're drunk." Suzie leaned forward. "Maybe that was the closest to the truth that she shared with you."

"Maybe, but it doesn't tell us anything more, does it? I really wish I had asked her more questions." Leanne put down her cup. "If only I had gone out there with her. I can't stop thinking about that. Now, to find out that Will stole from her and maybe was involved in her death. I just wonder what kind of friend I am that I didn't see any of this coming?"

"You can't blame yourself, Leanne. It sounds like Kendra was very good at hiding things." Mary locked eyes with Suzie. "Which means she must have had a lot to hide."

"She only ever mentioned that one betrayal? What about family, or friends from her past? Nothing about that?" Suzie asked.

"No, nothing. Whenever I asked about her family, she said she didn't have any. I thought it was strange, but I know not everyone has a good start in life." Leanne stood up from the table. "I should get back to work. I don't want to go over on my break on my second day."

"Thanks for your help." Suzie stood up as well.

"I'm not sure how much I helped, but I hope it leads to something. Thanks for the tea." Leanne turned and left the café.

"Not much more to go on, unfortunately." Mary stood up.

"If Kendra worked that hard to hide her past, then maybe she wasn't just running from something. Maybe she was running from the law. I think we need to be focusing more on her potentially criminal past. Do you think Wes would help us out more with that?" Suzie walked toward the door.

"I'm sure he'll do what he can. I'll see if he can meet us back at the house." Mary pulled out her phone as she followed Suzie out the door. She dialed Wes' number as she climbed into the car. After his voicemail picked up, she left a quick message, then drove back toward the house.

CHAPTER 24

Suzie and Mary arrived at Dune House to find Wes' car in the parking lot.

He stepped out as they parked.

"Wes, thanks for coming back." Mary hugged him. "I think we need to do some serious digging, and we're going to need your help."

"Of course, anything I can do to help, I will." Wes followed them toward the yard. "I noticed Jeanette went out for a run while I was waiting for you. I waved to her but I don't think she saw me."

"She goes into her own world while running." Suzie opened the gate and smiled as Pilot rushed toward them. He wagged his tail as he greeted each of them.

"It must be nice to be able to escape like that." Wes glanced back over his shoulder toward the beach before turning his attention back to Suzie and Mary as they walked inside. "So, how can I help?"

"I think we need to find out more about Kendra's tattoo." Mary settled at the dining room table. "It could be custom, and it might be the only connection to her past that we can find."

"That's a good idea, but I'm not sure how much deeper we can look into it. I know Jason ran a search through all of the missing person's databases and nothing turned up." Wes settled at the table beside Mary.

"You said Jason searched the missing person's databases." Suzie slid into another chair. "But isn't there another database for criminals? Don't the police document any identifying marks on them? Like tattoos?"

"Actually, yes. But there would only be documentation if the person had committed a crime," Wes explained.

"We think she might have. She confessed something to Leanne when she had a bit to drink one night, that she had committed a great betrayal, and she also seemed to have plenty of money with no real explanation for where it came from. So, maybe she stole it?" Mary raised her eyebrows. "There might be something there."

"Absolutely. I'm sure that Jason looked into it. Maybe he found a link but he hasn't mentioned anything about it, yet. Another set of eyes can't hurt. Let me start running a search now."

"I'll get us some lunch." Mary stood up from the table and headed for the kitchen.

Suzie walked over to the sliding glass doors and looked out over the beach. Jeanette ran into view. She looked at Suzie, then smiled and waved.

"Jeanette!" Suzie slid the door open and stepped outside. "Mary's making some lunch, come and join us."

"No, thanks, I have somewhere to be." Jeanette veered off toward the parking lot, then continued across the street in the direction of the dock.

Suzie stepped back into the house.

"Bingo!" Wes smacked his hand against the table and sat back in his chair as he smiled. "We've got her."

"What?" Mary peered over his shoulder at the screen. "Wes, what are you looking at?"

"Kendra's shoulder, actually. I used the picture of her tattoo, and I searched for a match in the police files I have access to. It took a little while, but it turned up the tattoo. It's associated with a small, tight-knit group who've committed a few robberies over the years. When I dug into them, I found some photographs of the members. There are only a few, and I thought I'd hit a dead end because all of them were men. But then I came across a female member." Wes pointed at the picture. "The tattoo on her shoulder matches Kendra's. Her hair is different, but I think there's a resemblance."

"Yes, there is." Suzie studied the photo.

"I think Kendra must have been a member of the group. Which means she participated in their crimes. Right now I'm running a records search to find out if there are any open cases suspected to have been committed by them. I can't find any links of any of the murder suspects to where the group appear to be based, or committed their crimes."

"When is that picture from?" Mary slid into the chair beside him.

"A couple of years ago." Wes glanced up at her. "I can't find her real name, though."

"So, Kendra belonged to a gang before moving here?" Mary tapped her fingers against her knee. "That does make things a little complicated, doesn't it?"

"Well, it wasn't really a gang. No more than six or seven people were involved in the group, from what I could find. They were known to pull off bank and jewelry store heists." Wes raised his eyebrows. "That might explain how she was able to fund her lifestyle without having a job."

"Maybe, but it doesn't explain why she suddenly moved here and decided to get a job at the library. None of this makes sense. Do you think someone from the group might have hunted her down?" Mary asked.

"It's possible. You did say that Lizzy advertised her yoga class with a picture that had Kendra in the background. Once something like that is on the internet, it can spread pretty quickly." Wes stared at the screen. "If she did something to cross the group, someone from it might have come across her picture and decided to get revenge. Or maybe one of the people they stole from did."

"Maybe." Suzie studied the photograph. "How long do you think the records search will take?"

"I don't have much to go on. It may take some time. I'll let you know as soon as I find anything." Wes looked between them.

"You have to eat." Mary pushed a plate toward

him filled with a sandwich and a mound of potato salad.

"Oh, that does look good." Wes met her eyes. "Where's yours?"

"It's coming up. Suzie, have you seen Jeanette? Do you think she wants some lunch?"

"She just went toward the dock, and no she said she didn't." Suzie looked over Wes' shoulder as well. "You said Kendra was the only female member? Does that mean that if it's someone from the group, it's going to be a man?"

"Probably. It's possible that there were more members that the authorities didn't know about." Wes set his phone down. "If there are any open cases, we might be able to see some updated information."

The front door swung open, and Josh walked through the dining room toward the living room.

"Josh, can you come here for a moment, please? Do you want some lunch?" Suzie looked up at him.

"Sorry, on a call!" Josh held up his phone as he hurried past them up the stairs.

"Okay, then." Suzie watched him go. "This is getting a little strange. When I tried to catch him last night, when he came home from work, he barely spoke to me. It was like he was trying to avoid talking to me."

"He's probably talking to someone about work or his new place," Mary suggested.

"Ladies, I have something." Wes picked up his phone. "We're in luck. There's an open case that's quite recent."

"What is the case about?" Suzie sat down in the chair next to him.

"It looks like a robbery from a couple of months ago. According to this, a bank was robbed, and the group Kendra was part of was suspected. But they were never able to make an arrest or recover any of the missing cash." Wes handed his phone over to Mary. "I'm sorry, I had hoped this would lead to something solid, but other than a few names, it hasn't turned up much. A couple of people died during the robbery, a Grace Wells, and a Tim Anders. I can't get any pictures of her, but I'll keep trying. I can't get specific details of the deaths, but the getaway car they were in was involved in an accident and burst into flames."

"Well, if Grace died, there must have been more than one woman in the group, as Kendra, or whatever her real name is, was still alive until two days ago. If we get this information to Jason, he might be able to see if any of the members have been spotted in the area," Suzie suggested.

"Good idea. I'll send him the information now." Wes looked up as Josh rushed down the stairs and headed straight for the front door.

CHAPTER 25

"There he goes again." Mary crossed her arms as she watched Josh walk out of Dune House. "Maybe he really is avoiding us."

"You were probably right earlier. I was just being paranoid. It's hard not to be with all that's going on."

"I don't know, Suzie. Maybe your instincts were right. It just makes me wonder."

"Wonder about what?" Suzie raised her eyebrows.

"Shawn claims he saw someone who looks like Josh out on the beach on Saturday morning. What if he really did see Josh?" Mary lowered her voice as she looked in Suzie's direction.

"You think Josh is lying about not being at

Dune House the morning Kendra was murdered?" Suzie leaned closer to Mary. "You think he's the murderer?"

"He claimed he wasn't on the beach, but how do we know for certain? I'm not accusing. I'm just pointing out the possibilities. Shawn says someone that looks like Josh was there. Why would Josh want to kill Kendra? I have no idea. But maybe he was there, and he's the murderer." Mary's eyes widened.

"But how did we not cross paths with Josh?"

"I don't know. It's possible he took a different route back. It definitely appeared that he stayed at Dune House the whole time."

"It did, I agree. I'm probably just being ridiculous to even consider this. But if our suspects are truly narrowed down to those who were spotted on the beach, or we know were on the beach, then maybe we've made a mistake by not really considering Josh as a possible suspect. What do we really know about him?" Suzie glanced over at Mary.

"Not much. But we do know that he's new to town, too!" Mary snapped her fingers. "It doesn't make him the murderer, but I definitely think we need to consider him a strong suspect."

"And not just him. I don't know anything about Shawn, either. I think it's time I speak to him face-to-face. I think it's better if I go alone. There'll probably be more chance that he'll speak to me if he doesn't feel like he's being ganged up on. He may not want to speak to the police, but he can definitely speak to me. I want to know if he really saw Josh out there." Suzie grabbed her purse, then glanced over her shoulder at Mary. "Let me know if Wes finds anything, okay?"

"I will. Be careful, Suzie. If Shawn was on the beach when Kendra was killed, and he has a sketchy past and doesn't want to speak to the police, it's possible that he's one of the criminals from Kendra's past." Mary searched her eyes. "Are you sure you want to go speak to him alone?"

"He probably won't even speak to me. But I need to try. Don't worry, I'll be careful." Suzie stepped out the door of Dune House and descended the steps of the front porch. She quickened her pace as she walked toward the dock. As she stepped onto the wooden boards, she heard a familiar voice.

"Suzie, did you come to see me?" Paul smiled as he walked over to her.

"Not exactly." Suzie greeted him with a quick

kiss as her heartbeat quickened. She doubted that he would be pleased with her intentions.

"No?" Paul looked into her eyes. "What are you up to, then?"

"I need to speak with Shawn face-to-face. I need to know if he's lying or not, because things are not adding up. I know you don't want me to, but I really need to."

"You know I don't want you to, but you still decided to come over here without letting me know, so that you could speak to him on your own? Suzie, you should know better than that. If you want to speak to him, I might not like the idea, but I will always be at your side to back you up. Let's go. He's on his boat." Paul turned toward the boat. "I think it's a mistake. I don't think he was involved in Kendra's murder, but if you absolutely have to speak to him, then we'll do it together."

Suzie's heart warmed as she saw the determination in Paul's eyes. He didn't want to stop her from making a decision he didn't agree with, but to ensure that she had his support no matter what.

"Thank you, Paul."

"Thank me after you meet him." Paul cringed. "He's not the most pleasant-smelling person."

"I'm sure it can't be that bad."

Moments later, Suzie held her breath as Paul introduced her to a burly man with a long, bushy beard, on a small boat.

"Ah, this is your girl, huh?" Shawn looked her over. "You weren't kidding about her, pretty as they come."

Suzie blushed and forced herself to take a breath.

"I just need to ask you a few questions, if you wouldn't mind."

"Oh, I do. I don't like answering anyone's questions. But a looker like you? I guess I can put up with it." Shawn smiled.

"Did you see anyone on the beach Saturday morning?" Suzie asked.

"Like I told Paul, I saw a guy with blond, curly hair. Looked about twenty," Shawn said.

"Do you know his name?" Suzie took a step toward him.

"No, I've never seen him before or since." Shawn shook his head.

"Is this him?" Suzie displayed a photo on her phone that she had found on social media of Josh and held it out to Shawn.

Shawn studied the phone.

"Yes, that could definitely be him."

"Then you must have been mistaken because the only person I know around here who matches that description is this guy." Suzie pointed at her phone. "And he claims he wasn't out there."

"Then someone is lying to you, gorgeous." Shawn winked at her. "But it ain't me."

"About what time were you out there?" Suzie asked.

"Let me see." Shawn narrowed his eyes. "I don't know exactly. I was out running for about forty minutes and was back about twenty past six."

"And you didn't see anyone else on the beach?" Suzie asked.

"Nope. Just that blond guy."

Suzie decided there was no use asking more about Josh. Shawn wasn't going to tell her anything else. She knew it would sound funny to ask Shawn if he had any tattoos, but she really wanted to find out if he was part of the group. That would change everything. She doubted he would be honest about whether he had a tattoo like Kendra's if he was involved, but it was worth a try.

"Do you have any tattoos?" she blurted out the question.

"Nope." Shawn chuckled.

"Don't you care about the murder being solved?" Suzie asked.

"Care about it? Sure. I mean, I didn't know her. She could have had it coming for all I know. I did my part. I told you what I saw. You're the one that's acting like I'm a liar. When I say a blond guy was on the beach, that's the truth. Not just my perception of it, it's the truth. I pay attention to everything around me."

Suzie's heart sank at the thought. Did Josh really lie about being on the beach? If so, why? Was he really the murderer?

"Thanks for your time. Try to stay out of trouble." Paul clapped him on the shoulder, then steered Suzie back toward the dock.

As Suzie felt Paul's hand against her back, she wondered if she should turn back and ask Shawn more questions. However, something inside of her told her that he wasn't the one who she should be questioning.

"I can't guarantee you that he's telling you the truth." Paul looked over at her.

"I know, but I'm glad we spoke with him. I have this uneasy feeling that I've had a blind spot this whole time." Suzie looked toward the street just in time to see Jason's patrol car heading in the direction of Dune House. "Jason might be going to Dune House. I want to see if he turned up anything. Do you want to come with?"

"I have to finish up a few things on the boat, but I'll be over later." Paul kissed her cheek. "Hopefully, Jason has good news for you."

CHAPTER 26

Mary opened the door as Jason approached it.

"I saw you coming." She smiled as she gestured for him to come inside. "I guess you discovered something important?"

"I'm not sure, yet."

"Jason!" Suzie hurried up the steps behind him. "Did you make an arrest?"

"Sorry, nothing as exciting as that." Jason stepped aside to allow Suzie to enter the house in front of him. "I managed to contact Molly and Michael."

"You did? And?" Suzie turned back to face him.

"And they claim they had an argument that morning. That's why they left early. Of course, that doesn't mean they didn't kill her, but the fact that I managed to get hold of them makes me less suspicious," Jason said.

"But they aren't in the clear?" Suzie asked.

"No, not completely. I also got a few more details out of Will, but I'm afraid they're not very helpful." Jason leaned against the wall just inside the house as he flipped his notepad open. "According to him, he did steal the bracelet. Though, he insists that it wasn't actually theft because by all rights he should be the co-owner of it." He looked up from his notepad. "I explained to him that an unwritten rule in a club doesn't amount to anything in the eyes of the law. But he continued to insist. He claimed that Kendra told him she intended to have the bracelet appraised that afternoon, so she had cleaned it up. He knew that she wouldn't be wearing it, so he waited for her to leave the house that morning to go to the beach to search for treasure. Once she left, he went into the house and took the bracelet. But he insists that he had nothing to do with the murder. Actually, if what he's saying is true, it gives him an alibi for the time of the murder."

"But no one can verify it." Mary met Jason's eyes. "Maybe he's lying."

"Maybe. I'm planning on looking into it more," Jason said.

"I think you should question Josh again, about his whereabouts that morning." Suzie didn't want to mention Shawn's name and betray Paul's trust and risk getting Paul into trouble with the other fishermen. She hoped Shawn would speak to Jason and volunteer the information.

"I was planning to. He claims that he was in his room asleep when Kendra was killed. But he can't prove it." Jason held her gaze.

"He's new to the area, too. He seems to be trying to avoid me." Suzie winced.

Wes walked into the foyer from the kitchen.

"As of now, that tip you gave me, Wes, about the group of robbers, hasn't panned out. I haven't found any evidence of the surviving members anywhere near this area." Jason looked over at him.

"That's frustrating. I'm sure there's a connection there, and it would make sense, since according to the open case file, there is a lot of money that has never been recovered from their last robbery. It would be a strong motive for Kendra's murder." Wes crossed his arms.

"It would be, but until I can make the

connection to someone in the area, there's just not much I can go on." Jason turned toward the door.

"I'm going to stop over at the train station in Parish. I know a few of the guys who work there. They would have noticed if anyone from out of town passed through. Sometimes you get more information from pounding the pavement." Wes patted Jason's shoulder as he headed for the door.

"I'll walk out with you." Jason followed him outside. "I want you to tell me everything you know about the criminal group that Kendra was associated with."

As the pair walked off toward the parking lot, Pilot stood between Suzie and Mary. He nuzzled Mary's hand.

"You need a walk, don't you?" Suzie patted his head. "What do you say, Mary, shall we take a stroll and try to get all of this straight?"

"Sure." Mary grabbed Pilot's leash.

Pilot bucked toward the door the moment his leash clipped onto his collar.

"I know, buddy, I know. You need some exercise." Mary looked over at Suzie. "I think I want to put my feet in the sand."

"Oh, good idea." Suzie followed Mary onto the porch, and they took off their shoes.

"It's always more relaxing to feel the sand between my toes." Mary started down the porch steps.

As they walked down the beach, Suzie ran through the possible suspects.

"At this point, we know there were five, possibly six, people on the beach that morning. Molly, Michael, Lizzy, Shawn, Jeanette, and maybe Josh, or someone who looks like Josh. One of them is very likely the killer." Suzie looked over at Mary. "But which one?"

"And, of course, there are the people that had possible motives, but we don't know if they were on the beach. Will has an alibi, but it's weak. Leanne had a possible vendetta. Do you really believe Paul's friend that Josh was out there?"

"I don't know." Suzie took a deep breath of the breeze that flowed off the mild waves. "Just getting some fresh air is making a big difference."

"Yes. Getting away from the house might help us work this all out." Mary looked down at her own footprints in the sand as they made their way over to near where Kendra's body had been found. She looked out over the water.

The wind blew gently across the surface of the

water. The waves sloshed forward over their feet, then retreated.

"I just hope we get some answers soon."

"Me, too." Mary felt something tangle around her big toe. She reached down to pull it free, expecting to find seaweed. When her eyes settled on a silver charm, her heart skipped a beat. "Suzie, look at this!" She reached down into the water. "It's a necklace."

CHAPTER 27

"A star." Suzie stared at the charm. "Where have I seen that before?"

"Jeanette." Mary curled her hand around the necklace. "It's hers. I saw it on her this morning. She must have lost it while she was out running today." She looked at the chain. "The clasp is broken."

"We better give it back to her." Suzie turned toward the house. "If we can get her to stand still long enough to give it to her, that is. She's always on the go, running around."

"At least we've managed to talk to her. Josh is definitely harder to pin down." Mary matched her pace to Suzie's despite the ache in her knees.

"You're right. Maybe Shawn is telling the truth

about Josh. Paul barely knows him, but he seems to trust him."

"Jeanette is there." Mary pointed to the large window that overlooked the front porch. "She's watching us." Mary waved to her.

"Let's catch her before she disappears again." Suzie hurried up the steps to the front porch. She threw the front door open. "Jeanette!" As her voice carried through the foyer, Pilot burst past her and began to bark.

"Pilot, it's okay!" Suzie looked over at him. Then the smell hit her senses.

"Oh, what is that?" Mary winced as she stepped into the house behind Suzie.

"Sorry, I'm just on my way out." Jeanette tried to push past them.

Suzie looked Jeanette over. She tried to work out why she smelled so bad.

"Wait, Jeanette, we found something that belongs to you."

"Yes, we did!" Mary smiled as she started to stretch her hand out to Jeanette. Then she froze. Her eyes settled on Jeanette's neck.

Suzie looked over at Mary, then followed her gaze to the silver star that hung from a chain around Jeanette's neck.

"What is it? I'm really in a hurry!" Jeanette looked from Mary to Suzie.

"Oh, never mind." Mary cleared her throat. "I made a mistake."

"Okay? If you say so. Excuse me." Jeanette brushed past Suzie and headed out the door.

Suzie exhaled as the stench of fish followed after Jeanette.

"What in the world did she get herself into to smell like that?" She waved her hand in front of her nose. "I guess we were wrong about the necklace. It's probably a pretty common charm."

"It is." Mary opened her hand and looked down at the necklace. "But what are the chances?"

"It's strange. That's for sure."

"What's stranger is how bad she smells. She's been near something foul." Mary shuddered. "No wonder Pilot barked. He doesn't want that smell around here, either."

"That's the second time I smelled something that bad today." Suzie's eyes widened. "The first time was on Shawn's boat. And Jeanette did walk across to the dock earlier."

"What would those two be doing together, though?" Mary sat down at the table. "I doubt there is a connection. She probably just got too close at the seafood market. You know how the tourists love to check things out there."

"Good point." Suzie settled in the chair beside her. "Now what? We're not closer to figuring this out. Now we just have a new mystery. Who does this necklace belong to?"

"We could post about it on the local community page and see if anyone is missing it." Mary snapped a picture of the necklace. "It really does look identical to Jeanette's. I wonder if somewhere nearby sells one like it. I can do a search of the picture." She tapped a few keys on her phone. Seconds later, she let out a startled gasp. "Look, Suzie. When I did a search, it brought this picture up. Wes sent me photos of the criminal group that he managed to find, including the one with Kendra. She's wearing the necklace in this picture. My phone identified the necklace in the photo as matching the picture of the necklace. It looks identical to the one that Jeanette is still wearing." She handed her phone over to Suzie.

"Wow, it does look exactly the same! But what does it mean? Why would Jeanette and Kendra have the same necklace? Maybe it's just a coincidence?"

"Maybe. But in the photo Lizzy took of Kendra, she isn't wearing it." Mary held up her phone.

"Interesting."

"Maybe she stopped wearing it because the clasp broke, and she kept it with her because it was important to her." Mary continued scrolling through the photos Wes had sent. Suzie looked over her shoulder.

"Mary, can I see your phone close up for a moment?"

"Sure." Mary handed it to her.

Suzie enlarged the picture.

"This woman, who is almost out of the frame, does she look familiar to you?"

"Only part of her face is in the picture." Mary studied it. "Wes said that he could only find one woman associated with the group. Kendra. But there's obviously more because there's also Grace, who died in a car crash. Maybe that's her."

"Maybe, or maybe she isn't part of the group, but the man standing with his arm around her shoulders is one of the men from it. He has a tattoo on his shoulder, of a dragon. Like Kendra's. Maybe she's his wife, or a girlfriend?" Suzie suggested.

"Yes, maybe." Mary looked up at her.

"Something about her does look familiar, but I don't know why."

"Picture her without the cap and sunglasses and with long, black hair." Suzie squinted at the picture. "Don't you think she looks very similar to Jeanette?"

"Jeanette?" Mary gasped and nearly dropped the phone. "Oh wow, yes! She does look like her! Do you think it's her?"

"I can't be certain. It's just a small part of her face. But maybe it's possible. If it is her, it might explain why she and Kendra had similar necklaces, or even identical ones. Maybe they used to be close. Maybe even best friends. They might have had matching necklaces." Suzie's voice filled with excitement. "Yes! It all adds up!"

"And if they were close, there's a good chance that Jeanette knew about the money being stolen. Kendra said she had betrayed some people. I bet one of them was Jeanette! Do you think Jeanette booked her stay with us before or after Lizzy started advertising? What if Jeanette saw Kendra's picture, and came here to hunt her down?"

"Are we really going with this?" Suzie looked into her eyes. "Do we really believe that Jeanette murdered Kendra?"

"I think so." Mary's voice trembled as she began to process the reality of the situation. "She was out on the beach. She might have been hiding, waiting for Kendra to arrive, so that she could kill her."

"Or at least confront her." Suzie sat back in her chair. "That's why she didn't have a murder weapon with her. I bet she only intended to talk to Kendra. But something went wrong."

"Kendra probably trusted her," Mary murmured. "She might have been shocked to see her, but she wouldn't have expected Jeanette to kill her."

"Wow." Suzie closed her eyes as she imagined the scene unfolding. "Kendra went to great lengths to keep her secret, and then one morning, it all came to an end."

"The only problem is, we don't have proof of any of this. We have a partial picture that we can only guess looks like Jeanette, and a necklace that's been in the water since Kendra was killed." Mary opened her hand and looked down at it. "There isn't going to be any evidence left to find on this."

"Which means there's a good chance that Jeanette is going to get away with this," Suzie said.

Mary took a sharp breath as the front door swung open.

CHAPTER 28

Jeanette rushed past them and up the stairs to her room.

"What do we do?" Mary whispered. "Should we call Jason?"

"And have him do what? Trust our hunch? He can't arrest her. We need to get some solid proof."

"Well, we can't just stay here with a killer in the house." Mary pulled Pilot close.

Pilot offered a quiet growl.

"Oh, boy, you never liked her, did you? You have good instincts." Suzie ruffled his fur. She opened her mouth to say more, but before she could, Jeanette bounded back down the stairs with her suitcase.

"Are you leaving?" Suzie stepped in front of Jeanette as she headed for the door.

"Yes, I'm sorry, but it's time for me to go. The way the investigation is going, it could take months or even years before the murder is solved. I'm sure no one expects me to stick around for that long."

Mary cleared her throat.

"Oh sure, no one would expect that. But it would be great if you could stick around just a little longer."

"Look, you've both been very kind. But I'm ready to move on." Jeanette tried to step around Suzie and continue toward the front door.

"We know about the jewelry, Jeanette." Mary blurted out her words, then glanced over at Suzie.

"The missing bracelet?" Jeanette narrowed her eyes. "I thought that was found?"

"No, not the bracelet." Suzie pointed to the necklace that dangled around Jeanette's neck. "A necklace like that. Kendra's necklace. The necklace that Kendra had with her the morning that you killed her."

"What?" Jeanette gasped as she took a step back. "What are you talking about? Have you lost your mind?"

"It's a star, identical to this one that we found in

the water near where Kendra was killed." Mary stepped up and held out the necklace in her hand.

"So what? I'm sure there are millions of star-shaped necklaces out there. It's not exactly a unique charm." Jeanette fiddled with her necklace. "You two have spent too much time watching true crime."

"You lied about hearing Kendra's voice calling out that morning. That's when I should have known. Kendra never had the chance to plead for her life, did she? She thought she was safe with you, because even after she betrayed you, she thought your friendship would keep her safe." Mary stroked Pilot's head.

"I have no idea what you're talking about!" Jeanette tightened her grip on her suitcase. "I've had enough of all of this. I'm leaving!" She took a step forward.

"I can't let you do that." Suzie moved in front of her again and held up her hands. "Jeanette, I know you didn't mean to kill her. You probably just wanted to talk to her. Maybe you thought you could reason with her? But she didn't react the way you expected, did she?"

"Stop it!" Jeanette glared at her. "I'm going to call the police if you don't let me pass. You can't hold me hostage here because you're a crazy person!"

"Yes, let's do that." Suzie held up her phone. "Let's call the police, and you can tell them your story about what happened to Kendra."

"Don't!" Jeanette suddenly smacked the phone out of Suzie's hand.

The phone flew out of her grasp, struck the hardwood floor, then slid across it in the direction of the dining room.

"Jeanette!" Mary gasped.

"Drop your phone, too!" Jeanette glared at Mary as she reached into her purse. "Don't even think about using it!"

Mary's mouth dropped open as Jeanette drew a small pistol out of her purse.

"Don't make me use this! Do you hear me?"

"Okay, Jeanette, just take a deep breath." Suzie lowered her hands some but remained in front of the door. "No one has to get hurt here."

"No?" Jeanette waved the pistol between the two of them. "Is that what you think? I mean, that might have been the case. All I wanted to do was leave. All you had to do was step aside." She gave a short laugh. "But it's too late for that now."

"Here, I'm putting my phone down, see?" Mary

dropped her phone on the floor. Her heart pounded as she met Suzie's eyes. "Please, just don't hurt us."

"I didn't want to. I didn't want to hurt anyone." Jeanette squeezed her eyes shut, then shook her head. "But you two ruined that. Now, I have no choice." She pointed the pistol at Suzie. "I have to get away. I can't let anyone stop me!"

"Wait," Mary gasped as she took a step toward Jeanette.

"Don't you dare!" Jeanette swung the pistol at Mary.

Pilot howled, then began to bark loudly.

"Keep him quiet!" Jeanette glared at Mary.

"Calm down." Suzie's sharp tone cut through Pilot's loud barks.

He sat down and looked at Suzie with wide eyes.

"Good, boy," Suzie reassured him.

"Okay, he's quiet." Mary crouched down and wrapped her arms around him. With the intensity of the moment, she didn't even notice the discomfort in her knees from being in that position. "See? He's just alarmed because he can tell that you're scared. We all are. I know you didn't mean to kill Kendra. Just tell us what really happened. We know that she wasn't innocent. We know that she stole money from you."

"Money? No, it wasn't only about the money." Jeanette stared at Mary. "Is that all you think she stole from me? No. She stole something far more precious than that." Her hand tightened on the pistol. Her voice shook as she continued. "I wanted her to know exactly what she did. I wanted to hear her apologize for it. I wanted her to tell me why, why did she do it?"

"And did she?" Suzie took a slight step toward her. "Did she apologize to you?"

Tears filled Jeanette's eyes as she continued to aim the pistol at Mary.

"No," Jeanette whispered the word. "No. She didn't apologize. She acted like we could be friends. Like she was so happy to see me. She acted like she had done nothing wrong." She groaned as she squeezed her eyes shut. "How could she?"

"You said it wasn't only about the money." Suzie's voice remained steady and determined. "Tell me what you mean, Jeanette. What did Kendra really take from you?"

"My trust. My friendship," Jeanette growled. "She betrayed me. We were friends since we were kids. She wanted to take part in the robberies. So, I got her involved with the guys through my boyfriend. She promised me she would split her share with me."

"But that's not what happened, is it?" Mary continued to hold Pilot close to her. "Because Kendra stole the money."

"Because Kendra, well, Grace, disappeared with all the money. But no one knew that she took it. We all thought she was dead." Jeanette glared at Mary. "She made it look like she had died in a car accident when she was driving one of the getaway cars. She was with Tim. They were carrying most of the money. I was so worried about her. The car burned in the accident, so the remains in the car couldn't be identified. It must have just been Tim. She must have killed him so she could take all the money. When the money came up missing, all of the guys presumed it had burned along with them. I felt so guilty that I didn't try to stop her from participating in the robbery. I was devastated. Heartbroken. I broke up with my boyfriend and moved away within a few days. But she was alive and well all along." Her voice shook. "She was my best friend. But she double-crossed me. How could she do that to me?"

CHAPTER 29

"Kendra didn't even apologize to me. She said that's life. That all's fair in love and war. She said it was a risk that came with the territory. Just like that, like it was nothing. But it was her fault! She was my friend. I trusted her," Jeanette shouted. "So yes, I grabbed that stupid metal detector and I hit her with it! I didn't think it would matter. How can you kill someone who is already dead?"

"You're right. You're absolutely right." Mary's heart raced. "It didn't matter. You were just settling a score. But Suzie and I aren't part of that, are we? You can't just shoot two innocent people. It's not who you are, Jeanette."

"You have no idea who I am." Jeanette scowled

at her. "I was so upset when she died. I was distraught. I barely kept it together. My running, the escape of it, helped me get through each day. But when I was on one of the fitness forums I belong to, I saw a picture advertising the yoga class with Grace in it. I lost my mind. I couldn't believe it. I couldn't believe she could really be alive. She had a different hair color. Her hair was short. She used to wear glasses, but she must have gotten contacts. She looked so different that I wasn't sure it was her. She wasn't wearing the necklace. But when I came here and saw her, she pulled the broken necklace out of her pocket and said friends forever. I couldn't believe it."

"The same one as yours." Suzie pointed at Jeanette's neck.

"Yes. My mother had bought us the necklaces when we were kids because we were so close, and there she was flashing it in my face after she betrayed me. I didn't want to wear the same necklace as Kendra anymore, but my mother had given it to me. I tried to convince myself that it was a trick when I saw her in that picture, that it couldn't really be her. That's why I came here, just to see. Just to make sure. I expected to turn around and go back home after having a good laugh at myself at how pathetic I had become. I thought that I wanted her so badly to be okay, that I was making things up. That, of course, she was dead."

"But that's not what happened," Suzie said.

"No." Jeanette lowered the gun some as she let out her breath. "Because when I arrived, I discovered it was her. I waited for her in the parking lot that morning. I took a picture of her as she left her car. I needed to be absolutely certain. When I saw some of her tattoo poking out from under her shirt, I knew for sure." She rolled her eyes. "I thought I would anonymously turn the picture in to the police, a tip-off. Or maybe send it to the guys so they could go after her. But a part of me still couldn't believe what she'd done. I just had to speak to her."

"What happened when she saw you?" Suzie eyed the gun as it swung a little lower in Jeanette's grasp.

"She was happy. The moment she saw me, she told me she had missed me so much." Jeanette smirked. "Can you believe that? As if we were being reunited by some miracle! As if I would welcome her back into my life! She betrayed me! She lied to me! She had to pay for what she did! I made sure that she did just that!"

"Yes, you did." Mary looked up at her. "You made her pay. Now that's over. Now you're in this moment. You have to think about what you're doing now. Suzie and I don't deserve to die, do we? You said yourself, we've been very kind to you."

"It's not personal." Jeanette raised the pistol again and pointed it at Suzie. "It's just what has to be done."

"But why did you stick around?" Suzie's voice trembled.

"I know it was stupid. I should have just disappeared the first moment I could. I was going to a few times, but I changed my mind." Jeanette cringed. "I really wanted to find the money. I wanted it. Some of it was rightfully mine. I deserved it for what I went through. For what she put me through. But the police were all over Kendra's place. I had to wait until things died down before I looked for it."

"Did you find it?" Suzie wanted to keep her talking. Hopefully, help was on the way.

"Yes, just this morning. I just managed to find it. Some of it, at least." Jeannette nodded. "It was in the floorboards of her house. They were told that was the best place to keep their stash. That it was the safest place to hide it."

A sudden knock on the front door caused Jeanette to jump. She ducked back and stared at the door.

"Who is that?"

"I don't know." Suzie looked toward the door as the knock turned into hard slams of a fist against the wood.

"Let me in!" Paul's voice carried through the front door.

"Did you call him?" Jeanette's voice raised as she aimed the gun at Suzie again.

"No, I swear, I didn't," Suzie murmured. "Please, just don't open the door. Just let him go."

Mary held her breath as she heard someone jiggling the sliding glass doors. She stole a glance in their direction and recognized Wes on the other side. She wondered if he could see them through the glass, but she guessed they were too far into the hall.

"Great! Just great!" Jeanette stomped her foot against the floor. "Not a sound. Not a movement. If they get in here, it won't just be you two that suffer." She glared at Suzie. "You brought this on yourselves. Do you want me to take them out with you?"

"No," Suzie whispered as she stared into Jeanette's eyes. "Please, don't do this, Jeanette. You made a mistake. You gave in to a moment of rage. If you explain what happened to the police, they will see that you weren't in your right mind when you killed her."

"No. Absolutely not. She ruined my life when she betrayed me, but I won't let her take my entire future, too. She deserved to die. I did nothing wrong." Jeanette glanced in the direction of the kitchen. "I already have my escape route planned. I just need to get out of here."

"Okay, we can help you with that." Mary stroked Pilot's fur and attempted to soothe him as the pounding and rattling continued. "Just let me answer the door. I'll distract them, and you can go out through the kitchen door."

"Yes, sure, like I'm going to fall for that." Jeanette rolled her eyes. "Not a chance!" She pointed the gun at Mary again.

Pilot let out a wild growl. He launched out of Mary's arms and straight at Jeanette.

Jeanette tightened her grasp on the gun.

"Pilot, no!" Suzie lunged forward and slammed into Jeanette's side in an attempt to tackle her to the ground.

A bullet fired from the pistol and sailed through the air just before Jeanette struck the floor.

The front door suddenly burst open.

"Suzie!" Paul charged in, his eyes wide and his cheeks crimson from exertion.

The splintered door hung from its hinges.

Suzie struggled to pin Jeanette down to the floor.

Mary wrenched the gun out of Jeanette's hand.

Pilot barked at Jeanette as he hovered right beside Suzie and Mary.

Paul grabbed on to Jeanette's legs and wrapped his arms around them to hold her still.

"Enough! It's over, Jeanette!"

Wes rushed in through the broken door. He ran his gaze across the scene.

"Is anyone hurt? I heard a gunshot!"

"We're okay." Suzie looked up as she and Paul continued to pin Jeanette to the floor. "It hit the wall."

"Thank goodness." Wes walked over to Mary who still held the gun in one hand. "All right, I'll take that."

"Jeanette killed Kendra." Mary's hand shook as she gave him the gun. "She's the one who did it."

"We know. Jason will be here any second." Wes rubbed her shoulder.

As if to prove his statement, sirens shrieked

through the air outside the broken door.

"How?" Mary looked over at Wes. "How did you know? If you two hadn't shown up, we might not have survived."

"Oh, I think you handled things fairly well." Wes smiled as he took her hand with his free hand. "Mary, you are the bravest person I know. I'm sorry that you had to go through this alone."

"I wasn't alone." Mary smiled as she met Suzie's eyes. "I was with the bravest person I know."

Jason stepped through the door with Beth and Kirk right behind him. He stared down at Jeanette, with Paul still holding her legs.

"I'm going to need a really good explanation for this." He looked from Suzie to Mary.

"She confessed." Mary met his eyes. "Wes was right. Jeanette knew Kendra from the past, and hunted her down for revenge. Now, Jeanette, you're going to pay the price for it."

Jeanette screamed as Jason handcuffed her.

"She deserved it! I'm glad she's dead."

"All right, you can tell me all about it down at the station." Jason hauled her to her feet. "Suzie, Mary, I'm going to need a statement."

"Oh, I'll tell you every single word!" Mary nodded.

CHAPTER 30

Jason escorted Jeanette to his car, while informing her of her rights. She kept her head low and mumbled something about Kendra winning, after all.

As Mary began recording her statement with Kirk, Suzie stepped outside.

Paul followed her, with one of her hands loosely held in his.

Suzie watched as the police lights strobed across the front porch of Dune House. She shivered as a cool breeze carried off the water.

Paul's warm arm curled around her shoulders.

She leaned back against him and closed her eyes.

"When I heard that gun go off, I thought I'd lost

you," Paul murmured just beside her ear. "I should have kicked that door in sooner."

"Paul, you arrived just in time." Suzie leaned up and kissed his cheek. "If it wasn't for you coming in at that moment, I'm sure that Jeanette would have gone through with her plans. What made you come here?"

"James, one of the fishermen, just got back from a trip. When I spoke to him, he told me that his son, Sid, had been visiting him in Garber. He had been walking on the beach around six on Saturday morning, so during the estimated time of the murder. He left to go home to Parish straight after his walk and didn't realize anyone had been killed. James had been out on the water, so didn't know what had happened. Sid didn't see anything relevant really, but guess what color his hair is?"

"Blond and curly?" Suzie clicked her fingers.

"Yes, so Josh was telling the truth," Paul said.

"And so was Shawn." Suzie turned to face him.

"About some things." Paul put his hands in his pockets. "I was near Shawn's boat, and I thought Shawn would want to know that the person he had seen on the beach wasn't Josh. But when I went to tell him on the way here, I saw Jeanette leaving his boat. I made him tell me what she was up to. He said that Jeanette bought a pistol from him. They knew each other from years ago. They ran in the same circles."

"So, it was a coincidence that they crossed paths here?" Suzie's eyes widened.

"Yes, I knew then that she might really be the murderer. The second he told me that he had sold her a pistol, I realized that you and Mary might be in a lot of danger. I put in a call to Jason, then ran across to Dune House to see if you were here. Wes had just arrived to see Mary. I filled him in on what I'd found out. When we heard your voices inside, and Pilot's barking, we knew that you were in trouble." Paul ran his hand across his face. "Suzie, I didn't know what to do. I didn't know if my knocking on the door would just make things worse. But I knew that I had to find a way to distract her and get to you. I thought about breaking the sliding glass doors, but I didn't want to risk Pilot getting hurt." He pointed at his bandaged foot. "That door was a bit thicker than I thought."

"You did exactly the right thing. If it weren't for you, she never would have been distracted enough for me to tackle her." Suzie glanced behind her at the shattered door. "But you do owe me a new door."

"I'll get right on that." Paul laughed. "Suzie, I'm just so glad that you're okay."

"I'm fine. I promise." Suzie wrapped her arms around his waist.

"Look at these two lovebirds." Mary rolled her eyes as she stepped out of the house. "Nothing more romantic than a crime scene, right?"

"Stop!" Suzie laughed. "I see that Wes hasn't left your side since he arrived. Isn't that right, Wes?"

"Yes, you're right." Wes draped his arm around Mary's shoulders. "When Paul told me what he suspected, I knew you both were in grave danger. I just wish we had been able to figure it out sooner."

"Jeanette definitely had us all fooled. I can't believe she killed her, and we never really suspected she was the murderer." Suzie cringed.

Mary looked over in the direction of the water as the sound of the waves in the distance filled the air.

"At least Kendra's murder is solved, and we can all feel safe when we close our doors tonight." Mary cut her gaze in the direction of the front door of Dune House. "Well, those of us that have doors."

"I'm going to fix it!" Paul gave a short laugh. "Just promise me that you're going to stay out of trouble. Any chance of that?"

"I can promise that I'll do my best." Suzie laughed. "But I do love a little excitement."

"Yes, I know." Paul sighed.

Pilot walked from person to person, receiving lots of pets and scratches, before he sat down at Mary's feet.

"Well, no matter what, I think there is one thing we can all agree on." Mary smiled down at him. "Pilot is the bravest dog I've ever known."

"Absolutely." Suzie grinned. "Treats for you, Pilot. Lots of treats!"

Pilot's ears perked up at the word.

Mary laughed and stroked the fur on the top of his head.

"Let's go, Pilot. There's plenty inside."

They all followed Mary and Pilot inside Dune House.

"I can't wait for things to get back to normal!" Suzie smiled.

"The problem is that normal with the two of you usually involves a little snooping and a lot of danger." Wes looked between them.

"What would life be without a little danger." Suzie laughed.

"Exactly." Mary smiled at her. "As long as we have each other, we'll be fine!"

The End

ABOUT THE AUTHOR

Cindy Bell is a USA Today and Wall Street Journal Bestselling Author. She is the author of the Little Leaf Creek, Wagging Tail, Donut Truck, Dune House, Sage Gardens, Chocolate Centered, Macaron Patisserie, Nuts about Nuts, Bekki the Beautician, Heavenly Highland Inn and Wendy the Wedding Planner cozy mystery series.

Cindy has always loved reading, but it is only recently that she has discovered her passion for writing romantic cozy mysteries. She loves walking along the beach thinking of the next adventure her characters can embark on.

You can sign up for her newsletter so you are notified of her latest releases at http://www.cindybellbooks.com.

ALSO BY CINDY BELL

DUNE HOUSE COZY MYSTERIES

Dune House Cozy Mystery Series 10 Book Box Set (Books 1 - 10)

Dune House Cozy Mystery Series 10 Book Box Set 2 (Books 11 - 20)

Dune House Cozy Mystery Series Boxed Set 1 (Books 1 - 4)

Dune House Cozy Mystery Series Boxed Set 2 (Books 5 - 8)

Dune House Cozy Mystery Series Boxed Set 3 (Books 9 - 12)

Dune House Cozy Mystery Series Boxed Set 4 (Books 13 - 16)

Seaside Secrets

Boats and Bad Guys

Treasured History

Hidden Hideaways

Dodgy Dealings

Suspects and Surprises

Ruffled Feathers

A Fishy Discovery

Danger in the Depths

Celebrities and Chaos

Pups, Pilots and Peril

Tides, Trails and Trouble

Racing and Robberies

Athletes and Alibis

Manuscripts and Deadly Motives

Pelicans, Pier and Poison

Sand, Sea and a Skeleton

Pianos and Prison

Relaxation, Reunions and Revenge

A Tangled Murder

Fame, Food and Murder

Beaches and Betrayal

Fatal Festivities

Sunsets, Smoke and Suspicion

Hobbies and Homicide

Anchors and Abduction

LITTLE LEAF CREEK COZY MYSTERIES

Little Leaf Creek Cozy Mystery Series 10 Book Box Set (Books 1-10)

Little Leaf Creek Cozy Mystery Series Box Set Vol 1 (Books 1-3)

Little Leaf Creek Cozy Mystery Series Box Set Vol 2 (Books 3-6)

Little Leaf Creek Cozy Mystery Series Box Set Vol 3 (Books 7-9)

Little Leaf Creek Cozy Mystery Series Box Set Vol 4 (Books 10-12)

Little Leaf Creek Cozy Mystery Series Box Set Vol 5 (Books 13-15)

Chaos in Little Leaf Creek

Peril in Little Leaf Creek

Conflict in Little Leaf Creek

Action in Little Leaf Creek

Vengeance in Little Leaf Creek

Greed in Little Leaf Creek

Surprises in Little Leaf Creek

Missing in Little Leaf Creek

Haunted in Little Leaf Creek

Trouble in Little Leaf Creek

Mayhem In Little Leaf Creek

Cracked in Little Leaf Creek

Stung in Little Leaf Creek

Scandal In Little Leaf Creek

Dead in Little Leaf Creek

Scared in Little Leaf Creek

Felled in Little Leaf Creek

Deceit in Little Leaf Creek

Secrets in Little Leaf Creek

MADDIE MILLS COZY MYSTERIES

Slain at the Sea

Homicide at the Harbor

Corpse at the Christmas Cookie Exchange

CHOCOLATE CENTERED COZY MYSTERIES

Chocolate Centered Cozy Mystery 10 Book Box Set (Books 1 - 10)

Chocolate Centered Cozy Mystery Series Box Set (Books 1 - 4)

Chocolate Centered Cozy Mystery Series Box Set (Books 5 - 8)

Chocolate Centered Cozy Mystery Series Box Set (Books 9 - 12)

Chocolate Centered Cozy Mystery Series Box Set (Books 13 - 16)

The Sweet Smell of Murder

A Deadly Delicious Delivery

A Bitter Sweet Murder

A Treacherous Tasty Trail

Pastry and Peril

Trouble and Treats

Fudge Films and Felonies

Custom-Made Murder

Skydiving, Soufflés and Sabotage

Christmas Chocolates and Crimes

Hot Chocolate and Homicide

Chocolate Caramels and Conmen

Picnics, Pies and Lies

Devils Food Cake and Drama

Cinnamon and a Corpse

Cherries, Berries and a Body

Christmas Cookies and Criminals

Grapes, Ganache & Guilt

Yule Logs & Murder

Mocha, Marriage and Murder

Holiday Fudge and Homicide

Chocolate Mousse and Murder

SAGE GARDENS COZY MYSTERIES

Sage Gardens Cozy Mystery 10 Book Box Set (Books 1 - 10)

Sage Gardens Cozy Mystery Series Box Set Volume 1 (Books 1 - 4)

Sage Gardens Cozy Mystery Series Box Set Volume 2 (Books 5 - 8)

Birthdays Can Be Deadly

Money Can Be Deadly

Trust Can Be Deadly

Ties Can Be Deadly

Rocks Can Be Deadly

Jewelry Can Be Deadly

Numbers Can Be Deadly

Memories Can Be Deadly

[Paintings Can Be Deadly](#)

[Snow Can Be Deadly](#)

[Tea Can Be Deadly](#)

[Greed Can Be Deadly](#)

[Clutter Can Be Deadly](#)

[Cruises Can Be Deadly](#)

[Puzzles Can Be Deadly](#)

[Concerts Can Be Deadly](#)

DONUT TRUCK COZY MYSTERIES

[Deadly Deals and Donuts](#)

[Fatal Festive Donuts](#)

[Bunny Donuts and a Body](#)

[Strawberry Donuts and Scandal](#)

[Frosted Donuts and Fatal Falls](#)

Donut Holes and Homicide

WAGGING TAIL COZY MYSTERIES

[Wagging Tail Cozy Mystery Box Set Volume 1 (Books 1 - 3)](#)

[Murder at Pawprint Creek (prequel)](#)

Murder at Pooch Park

Murder at the Pet Boutique

A Merry Murder at St. Bernard Cabins

Murder at the Dog Training Academy

Murder at Corgi Country Club

A Merry Murder on Ruff Road

Murder at Poodle Place

Murder at Hound Hill

Murder at Rover Meadows

Murder at the Pet Expo

Murder on Woof Way

NUTS ABOUT NUTS COZY MYSTERIES

A Tough Case to Crack

A Seed of Doubt

Roasted Peanuts and Peril

Chestnuts, Camping and Culprits

BEKKI THE BEAUTICIAN COZY MYSTERIES

Hairspray and Homicide

A Dyed Blonde and a Dead Body

[Mascara and Murder](#)

[Pageant and Poison](#)

[Conditioner and a Corpse](#)

[Mistletoe, Makeup and Murder](#)

[Hairpin, Hair Dryer and Homicide](#)

[Blush, a Bride and a Body](#)

[Shampoo and a Stiff](#)

[Cosmetics, a Cruise and a Killer](#)

[Lipstick, a Long Iron and Lifeless](#)

[Camping, Concealer and Criminals](#)

[Treated and Dyed](#)

[A Wrinkle-Free Murder](#)

A MACARON PATISSERIE COZY MYSTERY

[Sifting for Suspects](#)

[Recipes and Revenge](#)

[Mansions, Macarons and Murder](#)

HEAVENLY HIGHLAND INN COZY MYSTERIES

Murdering the Roses

Dead in the Daisies

Killing the Carnations

Drowning the Daffodils

Suffocating the Sunflowers

Books, Bullets and Blooms

A Deadly Serious Gardening Contest

A Bridal Bouquet and a Body

Digging for Dirt

WENDY THE WEDDING PLANNER COZY MYSTERIES

Matrimony, Money and Murder

Chefs, Ceremonies and Crimes

Knives and Nuptials

Mice, Marriage and Murder

Made in the USA
Monee, IL
05 June 2023